IMPATIENT WITH DESIRE

Impatient *With* Desire

A NOVEL

Gabrielle Burton

voice

Hyperion   New York

The excerpts from Tamsen Donner's letters on page 49, Hou 8 Donner, Tamsen to Elizabeth Poor, 1831–1832, June 29–Jan 26, and on page 107, HM 58153, Donner, T. to E. Poor, 1824, Nov.15, are reproduced by permission of *The Huntington Library, San Marino, California.*

Illustration of *Phlox carnea*, page 129, drawn by William Miller from *The Botanical Cabinet* (London 1817–1833), plate 711, engraving, 1820. File: Loddiges 711 Phlox carnea drawn by W Miller.jpg—Wikimedia Commons.

Illustration of *Delphinium speciosum* ("Shewy Delphinium"), page 194, *The Botanical Register*, Botanicus Digital Library, 1832, M. Hart. File: Delphinium_speciosum_1503.jpg—Wikimedia Commons.

Library of Congress Cataloging-in-Publication Data

Burton, Gabrielle.
    Impatient with desire / Gabrielle Burton.
        p. cm.
    ISBN: 978-1-4013-4101-5
    1. Donner Party—Fiction.   I. Title.

PS3552.U7728I57 2009
813'.54—dc22

                                2009030535

Hyperion books are available for special promotions and premiums. For details contact the HarperCollins Special Markets Department in the New York office at 212-207-7528, fax 212-207-7222, or email spsales@harpercollins.com.

Book design by Shubhani Sarkar

Map by Laura Hartman Maestro

FIRST EDITION

10 9 8 7 6 5 4 3 2 1

*This book is dedicated to
my husband, Roger,*

and

*our daughters, Maria, Jennifer,
Ursula, Gabrielle, and Charity,*

companions on this long voyage,

*steady in rough seas and smooth,
always providing a harbor.*

The Donner Party
1846-1847

Ocean

CASCADE RANGE

Oregon City

Columbia R.

Snake River

ROCKY

Missouri River

Bending River

Continental

OREGON TERRITORY

SHOSHONE

Little Sandy vote to take Hastings Cutoff

ARAPAHO

MOUNTAINS

North

Fort Hall

Snake River

PAIUTE

Wolfinger disappears

Snyder killed Reed banished

Great Salt Lake

Trapped

Donner Lake

Humboldt River

Fort Bridger

Sutter's Fort (Sacramento)

SIERRA NEVADA

GOSIUTE

WASATCH RANGE

Luke Halloran died

UTE

Green River

Hardcoop left

William Pike killed

San Francisco

Pacific

(CALIFORNIA)

MEXICO

Continental Divide

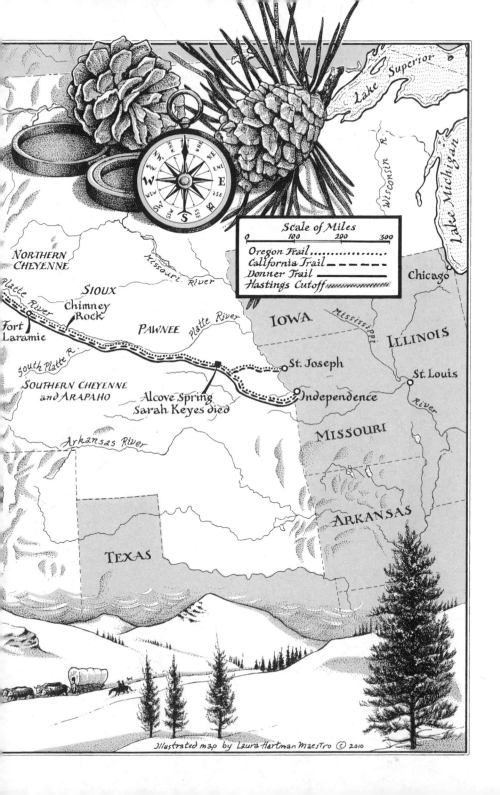

Lake Superior

Wisconsin R.

Lake Michigan

Scale of Miles
0   100   200   300

Oregon Trail ....
California Trail - - - - -
Donner Trail ▬▬▬▬
Hastings Cutoff ∿∿∿∿∿

NORTHERN
CHEYENNE

Missouri River

Chicago

SIOUX

Platte River

Chimney
Rock

Platte River

IOWA

Mississippi

Fort
Laramie

PAWNEE

St. Joseph

ILLINOIS

St. Louis

South Platte R.

SOUTHERN CHEYENNE
and ARAPAHO

Alcove Spring
Sarah Keyes died

Independence

River

MISSOURI

Arkansas River

ARKANSAS

TEXAS

Illustrated map by Laura Hartman Maestro © 2010

1846

Imagine all the roads a woman and a man walk until they reach the road they'll walk together.

I never intended to marry again after Tully died. It wasn't for lack of chances, but that's nothing to boast about. In Ohio, and in Illinois, even an outspoken woman like me has her pick of men. Most of the men were barely older than my Thomas would have been had he lived. Some women marry those boys, and I say to each her own, but young or old were not for me. I thought I had buried my heart with Tully.

I met George Donner in a cornfield, and the beginning wasn't auspicious. I had stripped an ear of corn for my students, discovered a larva, and put it on my finger for them to see.

"Corn borer larva," I said. "It's the larva of a moth. If unchecked, this little thing will feed on and destroy the hardiest crop of corn, potatoes, or beans."

As my students examined the tiny worm crawling on my finger, I looked up to see a tall gentleman in his fifties watching me intently. When I met his eyes, he said, "You need permission to be in this field, ma'am."

How many tall gentlemen have hectored me about one thing or another in my lifetime? I drew myself up to my full height, forcing myself to speak civilly because of the children.

"I am the teacher, sir. My students are gathering botanical specimens."

He considered that a moment, then said, "I'll still need to

know when you're here, ma'am. When the corn gets taller, I may have to send in a search party for you."

My students snickered. I am hardly taller than some of them, but I've never equated height with strength or virtue, and certainly not with good manners. I was about to give this gentleman a piece of my mind when I noticed how his eyes crinkled as he smiled, how benign and good-natured he looked, and yes, how handsome he was.

"Never underestimate the power of small beings, children," I said, and not breaking gaze with him, I squashed the borer between my fingers.

His smile grew broader, and he made a small bow.

"George Donner, ma'am."

I smiled and bowed back.

"Tamsen Eustis Dozier, sir."

Here in the mountains surrounded by snow, I have had occasion to remember that golden day, the corn rustling, the sun shining on all of us, the giggling children looking from me to him and back again as we smiled at each other, really one could not help smiling at this genial man. I remember writing my sister, Betsey, soon after we married, "I find my new husband a kind friend who does all in his power to promote my happiness & I have as fair a prospect for a pleasant old age as anyone."

The first part remains true to this day; there has never been a time I wasn't happy to see George walk in the door.

He always told the story of our first meeting the same way. "She came into my fields looking for specimens," he said and, after a pause, "and I'm the specimen she found."

For both of us, time stopped for a moment that day.

Now time has stopped in quite a different way. Instead of a golden moment being suspended, each day is relentlessly endless, relentlessly the same. During the day I move in ceaseless activity.

I have never had less to do and each day it takes me longer to do it, and still there are hours left over to fill. At night when everyone sleeps, I try to make sense of it all. Try to retain hope. Try to pass the time.

I must sleep. Sitting here at the table thinking or writing hour after hour while the others sleep or lying on my platform listening to their sighs and groans and caught breaths, it seems I never sleep. But then I awaken with dread, and it is morning with another day of interminable hours of unbidden intimacy.

We came here November 2nd, 1846. The day before, we were trying to outrun a sudden fierce snowstorm, my sister-in-law, Elizabeth, and I and our older children walking ahead of the wagon to spare the oxen, our eyes on the looming mountains. My little Frances was bravely trudging along, and I said to her, "Every step we take gets us closer to California." The huge flakes fell faster, thicker, and suddenly a sharp crack rent the air, I turned, saw the broken axle, the wagon heaving sideways, started running, screaming, "The babies," but George and Jacob were already pitching things out of the overturned wagon. They reached Georgia first, screaming, scared, but unhurt. Then Jacob uncovered Eliza and put her limp body in my arms. For a terrible second I thought she was dead, and I thought, I will not be able to bear it. Then she opened her eyes and began screaming. We all laughed with relief.

It was November 1st, my 45th birthday, and I gave thanks that Eliza was unhurt, and I did not have to hold a dead baby in my arms a third time.

All my life I never had enough time, and now I have nothing but time. My senses have become very acute. Several times here late at night, it seems I can even recall the precise sound of the corn rustling.

November

1846

Nov 9th 1846, Sierra Nevada Mtns,
still snowing

There are twenty-one of us here at Alder Creek in three shelters.

IN OUR SHELTER:
George Donner, 60
Tamsen Donner, 45
Elitha Blue Donner, 13
Leanna Blue Donner, 11
Frances Donner, 6
Georgia Donner, 4
Eliza Donner, 3
Doris Wolfinger, 19, from Germany (Her husband
   disappeared in the second desert—Oct 11–12?, 1846)
Uno, the children's dog

IN JACOB & ELIZABETH'S SHELTER:
Jacob Donner, 58, George's brother
Elizabeth Donner, 38
Solomon Hook, 14
William Hook, 12
George Donner, 9
Mary Donner, 7
Isaac Donner, 5
Samuel Donner, 4
Lewis Donner, 3

IN THE TEAMSTERS' SHELTER:

Samuel Shoemaker, 25, our teamster from Springfield, Illinois

James Smith, 25, the Reeds' teamster from Springfield, Illinois.

Joseph Reinhardt, 30?, from Germany (Augustus Spitzer's partner?)

Jean Baptiste Trudeau, 16, joined us at Fort Bridger—we say he's our factotum, because he can do anything

The second time I saw George Donner, he walked into my class-room with two other gentlemen. My thirty students, ranging in age from 6 to 12 years old, were reciting their times tables or working industriously on various projects. I was at my desk knitting. Mr. Donner, a step behind, looked reluctant, a little embarrassed; the other two men bustled with self-importance. The School Board Members. I had been waiting for them ever since my landlady told me that slanderous gossip about me was going around town.

"Children, we have visitors."

My students stood up. "Good morning, sirs." They sat down, folded their hands, and waited expectantly. I continued knitting.

The two officious school board members looked at each other with smug satisfaction. A smile played on George Donner's face.

"Is there anything you'd particularly like to see, gentlemen?"

Mr. Greene, a gentleman originally from the East who puts on airs and generally makes himself ridiculous, stepped forward and said, "We have heard that you knit during school hours, Mrs. Dozier."

"Well, now you can trust your eyes as well as your ears," I said pleasantly. "Please ask the children anything you wish. 13 times 7. The capital of Delaware. The inventor of the cotton gin. The main export of Brazil, the author of *The Last of the Mohicans,* the process of photosynthesis—"

Mr. Donner put on his hat and tipped it to me. "Thank you, Mrs. Dozier. Sorry to have taken up your time. Good day, children."

He steered the flummoxed board members out. Later, he

told me that he said to them, "I told you hounds you were howling up the wrong tree. I think she deserves an increase in salary, and I'm going to propose it next board meeting."

And he did. The first of many promises he has kept. George Donner is a man of his word, I was told by more than one person in Springfield before I even met him.

Nov 15th 1846

Jean Baptiste came back from the lake camp last night. He had been gone so long we thought he might have been lost. He said that when he arrived, a group of fourteen were just starting out to cross the pass and he joined them. They had to turn back at the end of the second day. He was very disappointed that they didn't even reach the end of the lake. He said it's much more difficult to walk in deep snow than he imagined.

They had more time to build their shelters so they're better housed than we, but other than that, Jean Baptiste says their situation is pretty much the same as ours. He says that everyone is confident that James Reed and "Big Bill" McCutchen will lead rescue to us soon. Their wives and children wait anxiously for them.

At the lake camp, there are sixty in three shelters.

The Breens moved into an existing cabin where an emigrant from the Stevens Party of '44 spent the winter. Jean Baptiste said that Mr. Breen calls it their "shanty."

IN THE "SHANTY":
Patrick Breen, 51, from Ireland via Iowa
Margaret Breen, 40

John Breen, 14
Edward Breen, 13
Patrick Breen, Jr., 9
Simon Breen, 8
James Breen, 5
Peter Breen, 3
Isabella Breen, 1

IN A LEAN-TO BUILT AGAINST THE "SHANTY":
Lewis Keseberg, 32, orig. from Germany, most educated
  man in our company
Philippine Keseberg, 23
Ada Keseberg, 3
Lewis Keseberg, Jr., born on the trail

ALSO:
Charles Burger, "Dutch Charley," 30, from Germany, our
  teamster
Augustus Spitzer, 30, from Germany (Joseph Reinhardt's
  partner?)

About 150 yards away, Jean Baptiste said the Murphys and Eddys
built a cabin against a large rock. In this cabin

THE MURPHYS:
Levinah Murphy, 36, a widow from Tennessee, Mormon?
John Landrum Murphy, 16
Mary Murphy, 14
Lemuel Murphy, 12
William Murphy, 10
Simon Murphy, 8

MRS. MURPHY'S MARRIED DAUGHTERS & THEIR FAMILIES
Sarah Murphy Foster, 19
William Foster, 30
George Foster, 4
Harriet Murphy Pike, 18 (her husband, William, 32, accidentally killed, Oct, 1846, along the Truckee River)
Naomi Pike, 2
Catherine Pike, 1

THE EDDYS FROM BELLEVUE, ILLINOIS:
William Eddy, 28
Eleanor Eddy, 25
James Eddy, 3
Margaret Eddy, 1

A third cabin was built a half mile away, a double cabin for

THE GRAVESES:
Franklin Graves, 57, from Vermont
Elizabeth Graves, 45
Mary Ann Graves, 19
William Graves, 17
Eleanor Graves, 14
Lovina Graves, 12
Nancy Graves, 9
Jonathan Graves, 7
Franklin W. Graves, Jr., 5
Elizabeth Graves, Jr., 1
    ALSO, A DAUGHTER AND SON-IN-LAW:
Sarah Graves Fosdick, 21
Jay Fosdick, 23

THE REEDS:
Margret Reed, 32
Virginia Reed, 13
Martha "Patty" Reed, 9
James Reed, Jr., 6
Thomas Reed, 4
Milt Elliott, 28, from Springfield, the Reeds' teamster
Eliza "Lizzie" Williams, 31, the Reeds' cook
Baylis Williams, 25, Lizzie's brother, the Reeds' handyman

THE MCCUTCHENS:
Amanda McCutchen, 25, joined us at Fort Bridger (Her
  husband, "Big Bill," went ahead with Charles Stanton in
  September 1846 to Sutter's Fort for help)
Harriet "Punkin" McCutchen, 1

ALSO:
Charles Stanton, 35, from Chicago, traveling with us
Luis and Salvador, Indians, "vaqueros," who came back with
  Mr. Stanton in October 1846 from Sutter's Fort with
  mules and food

We're not sure yet which of the three shelters the others
are in:

John Denton, 28, from England, traveling with us, carved
  Sarah Keyes's gravestone in Kansas
Noah James, 16, from Springfield, our teamster
Pat Dolan, 35?, originally from Ireland, friend of the Breens,
  most likely in their "shanty"
Antonio (?), 23?, our herder, joined us at Fort Laramie

· · ·

Altogether, eighty-one of us are trapped in the mountains. Here at Alder Creek, we are six men, three women, and twelve children. At the lake camp shelters, there are seventeen men, twelve women, and thirty-one children.

George and I have often talked about how the explorers went westward for knowledge or glory, the missionaries for converts, and the mountain men for adventure and fortune, but we of '46 have thought of ourselves from the beginning as bringing a civilization. We are the first year of the families on the Trail: a responsibility and a privilege that we have borne eagerly, indeed with pride.

When we were trying to hack our way through the Wasatch Mountains, we became aware of the liabilities of so many children, but that fact remained unspoken. Here in our grim shelter, the numbers laid out starkly on the page, there is no denying or ignoring their heart-sinking reality. As George and I worked out the ages of each for this list, we exchanged more than one look of dismay.

Sister,

Let me describe our shelter as for years I always described my current surroundings to you, Betsey, faithful to your instructions to "be particular with detail." We are in a clearing, three shelters in all, each at roughly the point of a triangle. When the storm forced us to seek cover, we put our largest tent against a great lodgepole pine to form the west side of our shelter. Then we drove posts into the ground and covered them with oxen hides. Erected in haste, it has served us remarkably well.

Inside at one end, we scooped a hollow in the ground, which serves as our fireplace. An opening at the top vents the smoke, but never all of it. There's always a smoky haze, and we're growing accustomed to our chronic throat clearings and coughs. It's night now, but night or day, along with the smoky haze, there are shadows, silhouettes, dark corners. When we go outside, the light hurts our eyes at first; then when we come back, we squint for a few moments until things become clear again.

At the other end of our shelter, posts and poles hold up crude wooden platforms we built out of weathered wagon boards. These platforms lift us off the wet earth, and we covered them with pine branches and blankets.

We divided one platform into two by hanging a blanket in the middle to give Mrs. Wolfinger privacy. Doris Wolfinger is a young German widow we took into our wagon after her husband disappeared in the second desert. She may as well be a hermit in a remote cave for all she is with us.

We made a rough table and two benches from wagon boards

and put them close to the fire. We eat there, I lave and dress George's wound there, Elitha sometimes reads her Dickens there. I sit there now, and most nights, writing. A giant pinecone, lit, is my "lamp."

Around the edges of the shelter we have several bowls filled with melting snow for our water. Close to the door, we have our slops and empty it outside daily except in the worst weather.

We almost always wear our coats inside over many layers of clothes, which I'm sorry to say, have not been washed for some time, a state I fear will continue. I suppose we are fortunate that it is too cold to sustain vermin.

Jacob and Elizabeth's shelter across the clearing is pretty much the same as ours except smokier and more pungent, although Jean Baptiste and I do our best to keep the vent open and empty the slops.

"The Indians do it this way," Jean Baptiste told George, and he instructed the men in making the teamsters' shelter, a kind of tepee, by covering triangulated poles with hides. Jean Baptiste is a godsend, and as good to the girls as if he were their brother. When the weather permits, he takes Georgia and Eliza outside and spreads out "Old Navajo," his colorful Indian blanket, on the ground. Eliza plops down and grabs one side, Georgia the other, and they begin rolling inward until they meet in the middle like two sausages. Jean Baptiste picks them up and props them against a log, where they watch him probe the snow looking for cattle or climb a tree looking to the west for the rescuers to come or simply talk to themselves in a private language they have made up. I could not manage without him. He finds firewood for all three shelters. He's of short stature, only five inches taller than I, but very strong. Jean Baptiste Trudeau is his full name. He is not sure where he was born. His father was French Canadian, a trapper, who was killed by Indians. His mother was Mexican and apparently died when he was very young. He says he doesn't remember her. I feel very tender toward him. He is a good boy, and his eagerness makes him seem younger than his 21 years—"almost 22," he said at Fort Bridger, where he begged George to hire him. "A dollar a day," George said, "and all the food you can eat."

Your sister

Thanksgiving 1846

We give thanks that we are alive and together. It stormed all day. We ate boiled oxen hides for supper. We have a little bit of meat left that I dried and parcel out every few days. I kept the children in bed almost all day because of the cold.

Personal History for the Children

I was born in Newburyport, Massachusetts, on November 1st 1801, the seventh child, the baby, of William Eustis and Tamesin Wheelwright Eustis. Thomas Jefferson was the third president of the sixteen states.

I was named after my mother, Tamesin, a feminization of Thomas, a name that, for some curious reason, lent itself to fanciful variations, Tamazin, Thomasin, Thomazine, Tamzine, Tamzene . . . Long ago, I gave up correcting people—even my first husband, Tully, spelled it Tamsan. I sign my name Tamzene, but most people have called me Tamsen, which was fine with me because it's what my father called me.

In fifteen years, my mother bore four daughters and three sons: Tamesin, Molly, John, Elizabeth, William, William, Tamesin. It was commonplace to give the name of a deceased child to a later child, as happened with my brother William and me. Some people believed we carried the spirits of our deceased siblings along with their memory, that we'd live their lives as well as our own. It is curious that William and I are the only travelers in our family, that we have never been content to stay put. Do the spirits of our older sister and brother, deprived of their own experience, drive us on to seek their adventures as well as our own? Or were we just born with wanderlust?

At the time of our emigration to California last April, only two of my siblings were still alive: Elizabeth (Betsey) Eustis Poor, nine years older than I, and William Eustis, two years older.

Betsey, my dearest only sister, has always been my confidante, unfortunately most of the time by letter. In the past William and I had our moments of contention—though I'm not sure he noticed—but we are on excellent terms now. When I left Springfield, he said, "Illinois is overcrowded and unhealthy. Don't be surprised if I show up at your door sometime." "That would give me a great deal of pleasure," I said from my heart.

I'm writing all this down, because today Frances asked, "What was Illinois like?" I was taken aback, but I spoke matter-of-factly about George's grown children back home, who were like indulgent uncles and aunts to them, the Sunday picnics, swimming in the creek, our farm when the fruit trees were in bloom. She and her sisters listened as if I was telling them stories from some book they'd read long ago and, worse yet, one they no longer had much interest in.

But why was I shocked? Each day, my former life seems more a dream to me too. I feel bonds loosening. I strain to hold on to my stepchildren in Illinois, Allen Francis, the editor of the newspaper, and my other friends we left behind, and most of all my dear sister, Betsey, willing myself to write letters I fear she will never read. The truth is it's difficult for me to hold on to anyone outside this wretched dwelling. The rest of the Party, seven miles to our west, might as well be seventy miles or seven hundred miles, although Jean Baptiste goes back and forth and brings us the latest dispiriting news. Even my blood relatives across the clearing require a bottomless attention I'm increasingly reluctant to give. Every day the weather permits, I force myself to walk across the clearing with Leanna to encourage my sister-in-law, Elizabeth, and my niece and nephews to gather firewood, to pray, to get *up* off their platforms. Every time we've been there this week, my brother-in-law, Jacob, was slumped at the table, his head in his hands.

Newburyport, Massachusetts, is a seaside town, and I grew up in a world that revolved around the sea. On the Trail every time a breeze moved the prairie grass someone would speak of it as waves. I can see they might think that, especially if they had never seen *real* waves. Prairie grass undulating is a pleasing sight, but it's to the great Atlantic as a minnow is to a Blue Whale.

My father was a sea captain, and he and my uncle and the other men in Newburyport were often at sea for a year or two at a time. My mother and the other women were in charge of home, money, and business. If the money Father left home ran low, Mother and later my stepmother made the long, difficult trip to Boston to sell whale oil used to light lamps, or barter it for goods we couldn't make at home. I begged and begged, and shortly after my 9th birthday, my stepmother and aunt let me go with them. I had imagined Boston many times, and though I was often teased for my runaway imagination, this time it had lagged far behind the reality. Immediately, the vibrant energy of Boston coursed through me. Everything was in primary colors, the sounds a thrilling jangle and din, and it seemed that everyone we passed hurried on her way to perform an important task. I saw that we were crossing Salem Street and turned with only one thought: Christ Church, Old North, where Father was a sentinel when he was only 15. I had only gone a block or two when it came into view, and though still some distance away I ran to greet it. And there it was, exactly as Father had described it so many times. As if happening that moment, I saw the two lanterns blinking from the steeple, One if by land, two if by sea, the horse's hooves slapping the ground, its mouth frothing, pealing church bells and town hall chimes, drumbeats and gunshots, carrying Paul Revere's warning from town to town: The Redcoats are coming, the Redcoats are coming. I climbed 154 steps to the top of the steeple and, when I looked out the window, was completely surprised to see my stepmother and aunt in the street below hurrying this way and that in agitation. I was sorry for the concern I had caused, but not at all for my adventure, and Father later whispered in my ear that he would have done the same thing.

A Ship Is Sighted

*W*henever a ship was spotted coming into Newburyport, my stepmother—and surely my mother before her, though I can't remember—grabbed the long spyglass and we all rushed behind her up to the widow's walk. All the ships had distinctive sails, and each captain his own flag, and what a happy day it was when she broke into a big smile. "It's your father's!" I was always the last to get the spyglass, and by then everyone was rushing downstairs to tidy the house, lay the fire, before we were off running to the wharf.

My brother John would lift me to the top of a barrel so I could better see the fishing boat rowing out to the incoming ship. When the rower drew close enough, he shouted, "What luck?" and we all held our breath until a sailor on the ship shouted back.

Oh, the relieved sighs, the whispered thanks of everyone when the shout was "All alive and well!"

Sometimes the shout was "Two men less." Then the hearts dropped, and we all waited in the heavy silence for the ship to slowly come to deliver its sad news.

Men of all ages strode down the gangplank, even the small ones seeming tall, their tanned complexions a stark contrast to our pasty winter white faces, bringing us the sights and sounds and smells of the world beyond Newburyport. A monkey with a gaudy red jacket and gold buttons perched on one sailor's shoulder; another had a screeching green and blue parrot. Then Father, tallest of all, swooped me up into his arms and onto his shoulders, and from that perch I saw the ecstatic reunions, I shook the paw of the monkey, feeling its viselike grip on my finger, and more than once from that perch, I saw at the side women and children weeping for their lost ones and was happy I was where I was.

I was long past riding on shoulders the day Father came down the gangplank, his face grave, and went directly to my aunt, whose face had already begun to crumble, and we learned that my beloved uncle lay in a watery grave. He had caught fever in Suriname and, although Father nursed him with a brother's tenderness for weeks, succumbed, and was buried at sea. For a long time, I never looked down at the ocean without thinking of those cold waters closing over Uncle.

In those early years at home before Uncle's death, everyone clustered around Father's leather sea trunk, peering at its exotic contents. On one homecoming, an orange was handed reverently from one to another to smell. Aromatic teas made the rounds. Then Father took out a beautiful opalescent shell and cupped it to my ear.

"Hear the trade winds, Tamsen."

I wanted to listen to the trade winds blowing forever, but William demanded a turn.

"Give it to your brother now," Father said.

William and I had a ferocious tug-of-war over the shell until he won.

Father looked at me with utmost sympathy. "If only you'd been a boy, you could be a sailor too."

"I will be a sailor!" I shouted.

Everyone laughed, except Father and me.

"Let her have the shell, William," Father said. "I have something else for you."

Father reached into his trunk and took out a small compass in a leather case, its face so shiny and splendid as to immediately capture my attention. Spellbound, I watched the needle move north, east, south, west as Father turned slowly around the room.

"West of the West," Father said, "lies a country of the mind."

December

1846

Dec 2nd 1846

*I*n the front of my journal, I tucked a copy of the March 26th 1846 advertisement in the *Sangamo Journal,* Springfield, Illinois. Last night, when George couldn't sleep, I unfolded it and read it to him, and we recalled the excitement we felt composing it at our kitchen table:

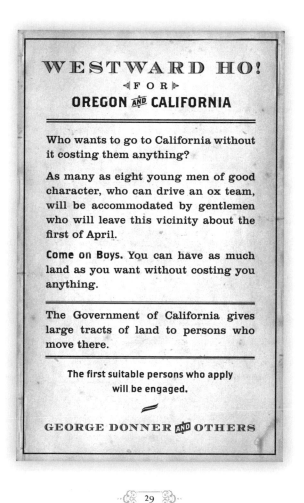

WESTWARD HO!

◄ F O R ►

OREGON AND CALIFORNIA

Who wants to go to California without it costing them anything?

As many as eight young men of good character, who can drive an ox team, will be accommodated by gentlemen who will leave this vicinity about the first of April.

Come on Boys. You can have as much land as you want without costing you anything.

The Government of California gives large tracts of land to persons who move there.

The first suitable persons who apply will be engaged.

GEORGE DONNER AND OTHERS

. . .

In Springfield, as every place else in the country, California fever was on the land. No more scrabbling for a living, out West the opportunities were unlimited, you could be your own boss. Good-bye forever to the hard winters and fevers and agues that sapped your strength before your time—you couldn't help being robust in the California climate. George loved to pass on the tale of the 250-year-old man who wanted to die and had to leave California to do it. "But when they sent back his body for burial," George said, his eyes twinkling, "what do you know? He was immediately restored to health!"

California was bigger than life!

My weekly reading group began discussing emigration as far back as 1844. We western folks prided ourselves on being as "up to date" as any Yankee, and as editor of the paper, Allen Francis had access to all the latest books as well as the letters sent back by those who had already emigrated. Gradually, as the months went by, our reading material became almost exclusively related to the pros and cons of emigration. Several of our more traditional members, who would have been content to read *The Hunchback of Notre Dame* until we had committed it to memory, found reasons to stop coming. I can't say they were particularly missed.

There were those in Springfield, as there always are anyplace, who thought only young, single men should go overland, that it was absurd and reckless for family men to consider it. But restlessness, risk taking, and adventure seeking are not confined only to the young temperament. Nor confined to males either. Though it's true that some women went only to keep their families intact, I was not the only wife and mother who thought emigration was the opportunity of a lifetime for the whole family.

.   .   .

The gentlemen got their eight young men, and a month later, we left Springfield, three family groups and our employees, in a little caravan of nine wagons.

George was a hale 60, I was 44. Elitha was 13, Leanna, 11, Frances, 5, Georgia, 4, and Eliza, 3.

George's brother, Jacob, 58 and in poor health ever since I've known him, hoped to spend his last days in sunshine. His wife, Elizabeth, was 38, and although I thought she was willing to go, I have come to wonder since. They took seven children: Solomon Hook, 14, and William Hook, 12, Elizabeth's children by her first husband, and George, 9, Mary, 7, Isaac, 5, Samuel, 4, and Lewis, 3.

Between us, we had six wagons and twenty people.

Our neighbors, the Reeds, had three wagons and twelve people. James Frazier Reed, 46, was a prosperous furniture maker; his wife, Margret, 32, suffered from migraines that James was certain California would cure. James claims to be descended from Polish nobility and more than a few people felt he was forever acting like it, but I always thought James knew his worth. (It's true that he might have been less generous in sharing that knowledge with others.) They took their four children, Virginia Backenstoe Reed, 13, Margret's daughter by her first husband and loved by James the same as Martha, 8, James, Jr., 5, and Thomas, 3, and Margret's mother, Sarah Keyes, 70. Mrs. Keyes was in poor health but refused to be separated from her only daughter, and James had his furniture factory build a special two-story wagon to make her comfortable. "Who will take care of her?" the tongues clucked right up to the day we left. "Not Mrs. Reed in her darkened room with her sick headaches. Not the cook, Lizzie, or her brother Baylis, the handyman, they're a fine pair, she's deaf and he's half blind, who else but James Reed takes servants to California?"

Thirty-two of us left Springfield that fine day, April 16th 1846, seven and a half months ago. One of our drivers, Hiram Miller—who is now one of our hopes—left the party in July to pack-mule to California. Surely he is there and has heard of our plight from James Reed, our biggest hope.

In high spirits, our little caravan headed toward the "jumping off place," Independence, Missouri, where we joined a large wagon train California bound. The expected time of arrival after leaving Independence was four months. We thought we would be in California before the leaves changed color back home. And now the leaves have changed and fallen, the winter wheat seeded, turned brown, and already dormant.

Two months after leaving Springfield, I wrote a letter to my good friend Allen Francis, the editor of the *Sangamo Journal*. Allen was publishing my letters for those contemplating the trip, and saving them for the book I am planning to write.

"I never could have believed we could have traveled so far with so little difficulty," I wrote. "Indeed if I do not experience something far worse than I have yet done, I shall say the trouble is all in getting started."

December 3rd 1846

Dear Betsey,

Georgia Ann Donner turned 5 today.

George told her five stories, plus one to grow on, and each of her sisters and I gave her six kisses.

Elitha also gave her a doll. Frances has had a doll, Dolly, since she was a baby, and Georgia has never paid one speck of attention to it until last week. "I want a doll too," she said and carried on about it until Elitha said, "Hush, Georgia. I'll make you a doll."

Had she had access to more varied material, I know Elitha's nimble fingers would have produced a prizeworthy doll. She singed and then scraped the hairs off a little piece of oxen hide, wrinkling her nose in distaste through the whole process, and fashioned it into a doll. She inked in hair, but the leather took the ink unevenly, so the little features on the face are askew, which bothered Elitha, but there wasn't time to start over. It is a queer little thing, but Georgia thought it was perfection, even if Elitha didn't.

Georgia asked me for a raisin cake like the one I made Frances on her 6th birthday in July. "All for myself," she said.

"I'll make you a big one in California," I said.

"All for myself just like Frances's?" she asked.

"If you want," I said.

She thought awhile, then said, "If it's *very* big, I will share with Eliza."

. . .

Of all my children, I worry about Georgia the most. At 5, she is no taller than Eliza, fifteen months younger. Because they're both dark with black hair and brown eyes, they have sometimes been taken for twins by the careless observer. But Georgia is petite and there is a frailty about her, while Eliza is sturdy as a small oak.

Georgia began life as a fat, rollicking baby and, as far as I know, never knew a day of pain almost her entire first year.

Then, one beautiful spring day, I was hanging clothes to dry, and she toddled up behind the new pony, surprising it, and it kicked out.

We would forever be thankful that the kick that might have crushed her only grazed her tiny leg.

George carried her in on a plank. We set the poor little twisted limb. She was in agony for weeks. The leg festered, and had to be cupped many times. The fever damaged her heart. She had a long convalescence.

"Georgia's just a spoiled little baby," Leanna has said more than once, and it's true that we all tend to fuss a little more over her. For her third birthday, George made her a special chair, a miniature of those in our house. It had a high, straight back, and for the seat, he wove light and dark leather strips into a patchwork pattern. Georgia jumped up and down, clapping her hands in delight, and George said, "You're not one bit happier than I was making it for you, Georgia."

Elitha fusses over her most of all. Age 10 at the time of the accident, she had been with Georgia just a moment before and blamed herself. For a time she was inconsolable. She seemed to finally accept that no one was at fault, but throughout Georgia's long convalescence, Elitha was attentive to her every want and, to this day, remains solicitous.

After her painful accident and long illness, Georgia didn't learn to walk steadily until the day her baby sister Eliza pulled her up and led her to the sandbox. Since that day, Eliza has been Georgia's staff, Georgia Eliza's shadow.

December 5th 1846

Leanna Charity Blue Donner turned 12 today.

When I showed interest and skill in botany at a young age, people frequently remarked that I was my mother's daughter, notwithstanding that Hannah Cogswell, whose herbarium and methods of specimen preservation were admired throughout the county, was actually my stepmother. And now I remark similarly about my stepdaughter Leanna. Of all my children she is most like me: intensely curious, adventurous, quick-tempered. Unlike me, she is tall and lean, can run a mile without stopping, and her handsome collection of marbles includes several glass beauties made in Germany that she won from overconfident boys.

There was a break in the weather, and we were able to go outside just long enough for a snowball fight, which invigorated everyone, and Leanna won fair and square.

George came up with the splendid idea of giving her a promissory note for a fine mare in California.

He had given her a feisty pony, Rouser, on her 9th birthday, and every morning on the plains, she and George jumped on their horses to ride ahead to pick a camping ground. One day he even took her on a buffalo hunt, "in the chase, Mother, close beside Father." Though they were both exhilarated, I said, No more buffalo hunts for Leanna. I would have liked to say, No more buffalo hunts for you, George, but I would have been wasting my breath. The meat was delicious, especially the hump, and a welcome addition to the monotonous baked beans and pickles, but not worth the danger to me.

Unlike her older sister, Elitha, who rides elegantly and is one with the horse, Leanna rides as she does everything: powerfully, pell-mell, full-out.

No one spoke of her beloved Rouser, whom we had to leave behind, Leanna sobbing at the back wagon cover as she watched her pony growing small, smaller, until it was gone.

December 8th 1846

Yesterday, Milt Elliott came over from the lake camp, and I cannot tell you what a tonic it was for us to see that dear open face. Milt has been with us since Springfield, ever faithful to his employer, James Reed, and to us. George has known Milt since he was a little boy, and though they're not blood relatives, Milt was only one of many young men in Springfield who would do anything for his "Uncle George."

Milt says Mrs. Reed and the children and Mrs. McCutchen are doing as well as can be expected. More than two months now since James Reed was banished and rode off on one horse with Walter Herron, and nearly that long since Mr. Stanton brought back word that "Big Bill" McCutchen was recovering at Sutter's Fort.

When the weather breaks, Milt and Charles Stanton and William Eddy and others are going to try again to cross. We wrote out a list of things for Milt to bring back for us. Unable to rouse Jacob to sign the promissory note, George signed for him.

We have requested horses, mules, and flour, promising to pay for them in California. Outside, I privately asked Milt to also bring back unguent, bandages, and whiskey.

"You hankering for a drink, Mrs. Donner?" he teased, and I laughed and said, "Strictly medicinal purposes, Milt."

December 11th 1846

*B*efore we could hardly start counting the days, Milt appeared at our door again. Due to soft snow and drifts, he and the others didn't get as far as the last attempt. "Don't worry, Uncle George," he said, "we have another plan. We're making snowshoes. Graves saw them in Vermont and Stanton in upstate New York."

He handed me a letter from Mr. Stanton—addressed to "Donnersville," which made George and me smile wryly. Charles Stanton traveled in our wagons from Independence on, and a more congenial traveling companion there never was. He was as keen on botanizing as I, and we spent many a pleasant nooning together on the prairies with their vast grasslands and profusion of wildflowers. One day we found wild peas, and my sister-in-law, Elizabeth, was ecstatic.

In his letter, Mr. Stanton asked if we had any tobacco and if he could borrow my compass. "Graves is coming right back for his family," he wrote, "and he'll bring your compass back to you."

I can't lend him my compass, I thought wildly, I'll need it . . .

"Mrs. Donner?" Milt said, and I realized he was waiting for my answer. George was looking at me too. I couldn't think what to say.

"We can spare some tobacco," George said and got up to get it.

Dec 21st 1846

A storm prevented Milt from leaving. He was with us nine days, staying in the teamsters' hut. He sat at Jacob's bedside with us all night long, George holding his brother's hand until Jacob died, and he helped us bury Jacob in the whirling snow. He was there when our teamster Samuel Shoemaker died.

Night before last, poor Milt, shaken and scared by the almost simultaneous deaths of Jacob and Samuel, and the moribund condition of our other teamster James Smith, wanted to leave for the lake camp immediately. It was with some difficulty that George persuaded him to wait until daybreak.

We sat by the fire, and when I handed him a cup of coffee, his hands shook uncontrollably. I had to hold it for him to drink. "Sammy won the calf-lifting contest four years straight," he said. "Nobody could beat Sammy."

"We don't understand it either, Milt," I said. "Young, healthy men like yourself, and we have been unable to rally them. They don't seem to want to live."

"Are we all gonna die like Mrs. Donner said?" Milt blurted out, saying aloud my sister-in-law's words that had been thundering unspoken in the air since Jacob's burial.

"Of course not," I started, but there was a crash on the stairs as if someone had fallen, and we jumped up just as Joseph Reinhardt, the German staying in the teamsters' shelter, staggered into our shelter and collapsed. Milt dragged him to a platform.

Although she rarely comes out volitionally, Mrs. Wolfinger instantly appeared from behind her blanket.

Mr. Reinhardt opened his eyes, looked wildly at George. "Wolfinger, Wolfinger. I'm sorry . . ."

George leaned close. "Who killed Wolfinger?"

"Have mercy, O God have mercy, O Gott . . . ," Mr. Reinhardt said over and over, thrashing back and forth. He lapsed into German. "Ich komme in die Hölle . . ."

"Ja," Mrs. Wolfinger spit out and went back behind her blanket. George tried to soothe Mr. Reinhardt without success until the thrashing and babbling stopped. I suddenly realized that Leanna and Elitha were sitting up on their platforms and Frances stood nearby, wide-eyed. "Mr. Reinhardt has died," I said. "Go back to bed, Frances. All of you go to sleep. You need your sleep."

Even in death, Mr. Reinhardt's distress remained on his contorted face. Milt helped us wrap him in a blanket and drag the body up the stairs and out into the snow behind the shelter, looking stunned and bewildered the whole time. This time, even though dawn was two hours away, neither George nor I could persuade him to stay the rest of the night in the teamsters' wigwam—"Not with James Smith, Mrs. Donner"—or even on hides near our fire.

Milt gone, the children finally asleep, George and I sat by the fire, lost in our thoughts. George met my eyes, gestured toward Mrs. Wolfinger's blanket, and whispered, "She asleep?"

I nodded.

"I didn't know how to comfort Reinhardt," he said. "He was such a troubled soul. Was he raving or confessing?"

"He said he was going to Hell," I said.

I opened the Bible to write Mr. Reinhardt's name.

DEATHS ON THE TRAIL

Sarah Keyes, 70, d. May 26th 1846 at Alcove Springs, Kansas. Margret Reed's mother. Peacefully of old age, her daughter, son-in-law, and grandchildren around her.

Luke Halloran, 25, d. Aug 25th 1846 on the south side of Salt Lake, of tuberculosis, traveling in our wagon from Little Sandy, the "Parting of the Ways."

John Snyder, 25, d. Oct. 5th 1846 in Nevada territory. Franklin Graves's teamster, "Driver par Excellence," accidentally killed by James Reed.

Hardcoop, 60?, d. Oct 7–8th? 1846 in the desert. Originally from Belgium, one daughter there, name unknown. Abandoned.

Mr. Wolfinger, 22–26?, d. Oct ? 1846 between Humboldt Sink and Truckee River. Disappeared. Foul play suspected. From Germany, husband of Doris.

William Pike, 32, d. Oct 26th 1846 in Truckee Meadows. Husband and father, Levinah Murphy's son-in-law, traveling with the Murphy clan. Accidentally killed by his brother-in-law.

DEATHS IN THE MOUNTAINS

Jacob Donner, 58, d. Dec 16th 1846 at Alder Creek. Born in North Carolina, recently of Springfield, Illinois, beloved husband, father, brother.

Samuel Shoemaker, 25, d. Dec 17th 1846 at Alder Creek. Donner teamster from Springfield. Calf-lifting champion.

James Smith, 25, d. Dec 20th 1846 at Alder Creek. Reed teamster from Springfield.

Joseph Reinhardt, 30?, d. Dec 20th 1846 at Alder Creek. From Germany, partner with Augustus Spitzer?

Dec 22nd 1846

When we came here, we had some coffee, tea, and a little bit of sugar that I saved for Frances, Georgia, and Eliza. Every night when I put them to bed, I gave them a tiny lump. Every night Uno, on the platform at their feet, waited eagerly for Georgia to finger the fleck of sugar dissolving on her tongue, and hold out her finger for him to lick thoroughly.

Tonight, Georgia stuck out her tongue for her lump.

"There is no more, Georgia," I said.

Her big eyes filled with tears.

"Can you get us some at the store?" Eliza asked.

"California has bags of sugar on the ground," Frances said.

Whimpering, they finally fell asleep.

Ears pricked, Uno waited for his sugar in vain.

Our Hopes

1. James Reed, his wife and four children at the lake camp waiting for him.
2. "Big Bill" McCutchen, his wife and baby girl at the lake camp waiting for him.
3. Hiram Miller, our teamster from Springfield, who joined a pack mule train in July because the wagon train was too slow for him. He will have heard of our plight from Mr. Reed and Mr. McCutchen. Hiram has no family here but is especially fond of "Uncle George."
4. Walter Herron, James Reed's teamster, who rode off with him after James was banished. We could spare only one horse, and Walter said, "I don't want to go out there, Mr. Donner." "You're his teamster, Walter," George said.

In that order, I think, we have four hopes just across the mountains to the west, who will tell others, may already be forming relief parties.

Do they look east at the mountaintop and imagine us as we look west and imagine them?

Later

George just had a terrible thought. Neither Reed nor McCutchen will know we lost almost all the cattle in the snow. They will figure we have enough food to last till spring.

Dec 23rd 1846

The snowshoers didn't wait for Milt to get back, and Mr. Stanton left without the tobacco and never knew I didn't lend him my compass. Jean Baptiste said that fifteen of them started out to cross the mountains December 16th.

"They sawed oxbows into strips, keeping the curved shape," I told the children. "Then they cut hides into narrow strips and wove them like this. Something like your little chair seat, Georgia." I dashed off a sketch of snowshoes for the children. "Wasn't that clever of them? I saw snowshoes in Maine. You can walk right on top of snow—"

"Where's my special chair?" Georgia asked.

"It's in the third wagon that has all the things we won't need until California," I said, then continued. "Five women, eight men, and two boys went. Three of the women were nursing and their milk dried up. They've gone to get milk for their children."

"Oh, how quickly I'd give my green velvet dress and my green Moroccan leather shoes for one glass of milk," Elitha said. "A *half* glass of milk, white and thick and creamy, little bits of butter—"

"Mr. Stanton has already made the trip to Sutter's Fort and back, so he knows the way," I said. "Rescue will be coming soon."

Now we have five hopes.

I've already told you, Betsey, how agreeable a traveling companion I found Mr. Stanton, but I also found him a man of great integrity.

In August, when we found the first note from Lansford Hastings—"Weber Canyon bad. Make camp and send someone ahead. I will return to lead you."—Mr. Stanton was the first to volunteer. "Pick a married man, so we know he'll come back," Mr. Breen said, and Mr. Stanton colored. He rode off with James Reed and William Pike, and we waited four long days until James Reed reappeared alone. Mr. Stanton's and Mr. Pike's horses had broken down, and James on a horse borrowed from Hastings brought bad news. Lansford Hastings was not coming back to lead us; the company before us that he was leading had barely gotten through the Weber Canyon, and they had many more men than we, far fewer women and children. Our only possible route was through the Wasatch Mountains.

We set off on a vague course that James had tried to blaze. There was no road, not even a trail. A week later, Mr. Stanton and Mr. Pike, who had been wandering through the wilderness for days trying to find us, limped up on foot to deliver the dispiriting news that the road we had been hacking out was leading straight to an impassable gorge. Again, we had to turn around and start over.

In September, when it became obvious that our supplies were inadequate, Mr. Stanton was again the first to volunteer to go ahead to Sutter's Fort for help. This time, Mr. Breen said nothing about married men. "Big Bill" McCutchen volunteered to go with him, the giant McCutchen and the diminutive Stanton making a funny duo as they rode off on one horse.

In October, we had our first cheerful day in a long time when Mr. Stanton came clattering down the trail toward us with pack mules laden with food from Captain Sutter and two vaqueros, Luis and Salvador, and news that James Reed was nearly to Sutter's Fort. "Big Bill" McCutchen, too ill to travel, was recouping his strength at Sutter's Fort.

With no blood ties to our company, only his honor guiding him, Mr. Stanton has already come back twice. I know he will come back again this time.

Godspeed, Mr. Stanton.

Dear Betsey,

Christmas has come and gone. We ate the loathsome oxen hides in silence. Across the table, I looked at Georgia's little pinched face, Frances's golden curls dull and lank . . . my head whirling with pictures and voices: "Who wants to crack walnuts, you'll spoil your supper with all that gingerbread, save room for the hot mince pies, Now children, just because it's roast turkey you don't have to gobble gobble, Father, you say that every year." When Frances asked me to tell a story about other Christmases, I said, "Not now." Her face fell, and I said, "Maybe later."

I think I told myself that speaking of those happy times would only bring the children more pain. It might just as well have brought them hope that those times will come again. The truth is, Betsey, I forgot that Frances asked me. All I could think of was a long-ago Christmas tree with candles snuffed out, keening alone in the dark, tears soaking my letter to you:

Jan, 1832

I have lost that little boy I loved so well. He died the 28th of September. I have lost my husband who made such a large share of my happiness. He died on the 24th of December. I prematurely had a daughter which died on the 18th of Nov. O my sister, weep with me if you have tears to spare.

I remember writing those words after Tully died, thinking I would never recover. Margret Reed lost her first husband too, and lost a little boy three months before we left Illinois, and now she may have lost another husband—nearly three months since James was banished. Her children did not eat hides on Christmas Day. Jean Baptiste spent Christmas at the other camp and brought the story back today. Weeks back, Margret planned—burying bits of food deep in a snow mound—and early Christmas morning, she began her surprise.

I can see only too clearly the Reed children cluster about the small kettle. Their faces bend close to suck in the steam, the smell of the unexpected feast. Their cabin fills with unfamiliar sounds—the noise of excited children, not like mine, who lie languidly on their racks and have to be cajoled to get up, go outside—little Jimmy Reed shrieks with joy, "There's *mine*," as a small white bean surfaces, bobbling in the swirling broth.

Margret Reed. Always suffering from "sick headaches" back in Springfield, and the day James was banished, his head dripping with blood from Snyder's bullwhip, Margret too distraught to dress his wounds, leaving Virginia, a slip of girl, to attend properly to James. . . . God forgive me, forgive me, Margret. Margret was wounded too, "down came the stroke full upon her," James said with anguish, the men gathering to hang him: How would I have responded? We all came here strangers to ourselves.

Margret Reed celebrated Christmas properly. I am awed and shamed.

In the corner of the cabin, Jean Baptiste said, the smaller Graves children watched the four Reed children sitting around the table on their best behavior as their mother ladled out the meager feast.

"Tripe! And salt pork! And beans! Tell us again where it came from, Mother," Virginia said.

"Weeks back I hid it for today," Margret said.

"It's a Christmas miracle!" little Patty said.

A half-inch wedge of salt pork, a tiny bit of tripe, a handful of beans. They all bowed their heads. "We give thanks for this bounty," Margret said. "We pray for your father's safety on this Christmas Day. Now eat slowly, children. There is plenty for all."

January

1847

Jan 4th 1847, rained all night,
snow beginning now

Jean Baptiste told me that the last thing Samuel Shoemaker said before he died on his platform in the dark, dank shelter, was "Roast pork, Mother! And sweet potato pie! Oh, Mother! You've made all my favorites." Then he closed his eyes, a rapturous smile on his face.

Our thoughts are consumed with food. We dream about food. My sister-in-law, Elizabeth, endlessly comes up with more and more elaborate recipes to cook until I think I will go mad. When the children talk about food, I discourage it. "A rasher of bacon," Elitha blurts out. "Oh, wouldn't a rasher of fatty bacon taste heavenly—" "You *hated* fatty bacon," Leanna says angrily, "Mother had to practically cook it to char to get you to taste it," and Elitha bursts into tears, lamenting all the food she wasted. "We'll have plenty of bacon in California," I say. Then twenty minutes or an hour later, Elitha says, "A fried egg swimming in that bacon grease. That has to be the most perfect food—" "Just keep quiet!" Leanna yells. "Please, children," I say.

We lost most of the cattle in the snow, and the few we found and immediately butchered were so scrawny their meat was quickly gone. For some time we have subsisted on oxen hides.

Today we prepared the oxen hides as usual. I try to keep the children to a strict routine, organizing their days to give them some shape and sense of time passing. By and large, they don't balk, though Leanna, impatient like me, sometimes narrows her eyes and hesitates just long enough to tell me she's going along now, but . . . Exactly as I acted at her age.

I scored and cut the hide into strips. Elitha passed a candle flame back and forth over a strip, singeing the hairs, her nostrils flaring at the acrid smell. She passed the strip to Leanna, who scraped the singed strip with a knife. "I'm way ahead of you," she said. There is not a task in the world that Leanna cannot make into a competition.

Elitha rolled her eyes. "Just be sure you get all those little bits, Leanna," she said in her big sister, bossy voice. "It's even more disgusting with hairs."

"You'll never catch up," Leanna said, tossing her finished piece into a big pot on the fire.

"I *loathe* and *detest* hides," Elitha said. "When we get to California, I will *never* eat jelly again!"

"Be glad we have them," George said.

Leanna snorted, but I pretended not to notice. He's right of course; hides are the only thing between us and starvation, but *glad* does seem a little too cheerful and lighthearted for that gray, glutinous mass bubbling on the fire, basically a pot of hot glue.

I cut, Elitha passed the candle flame over, Leanna scraped. "You're not getting them all, Leanna," Elitha said again. "Get them all out . . ."

"Get all the feathers out, especially the little pinfeathers," I say, handing the unplucked pheasants to Elitha and Leanna. "We'll enjoy these at nooning." I turn back to the brace of pheasants George shot this morning, necks wrung, one plucked on my improvised butcher board. Leanna starts right in yanking feathers out, but Elitha grimaces and hangs back. With a cleaver, I crack the breastbone of the plucked pheasant, open it, remove the heart and liver. Elitha blanches.

"Don't be squeamish, Elitha," I say. "It's not an attractive trait. The

good Lord put this abundance on earth for us." I butcher the bird quickly, as I have butchered hundreds before it. "Do you know what the Indians say, Elitha? They say, 'We thank this bird that gave its life so we might have food.'"

I looked at the tough, hairy oxen hide in front of me, the knife in my hand, my mouth watering at the thought of those plump pheasants we ate so matter-of-factly. Would that we had a bird to thank today.

Jan 8th 1847

*T*oday, after Elitha marked the big red *X* on the calendar I made, I pointed four days back, to January 4th. "Jean Baptiste said that Margret and Virginia Reed, Milt Elliott, and their cook, Lizzie, set out here to cross the mountains on foot."

"Mrs. Reed?" George said.

I saw his astoundment and would have privately shared it before hearing about her Christmas feast. I nodded.

"That's sheer lunacy," George said.

I glanced over at Frances, Georgia, and Eliza in bed, playing their game of "cards," withdrawn from our conversation by the fire. Frances triumphantly laid down a card with a moon painted on it, and Georgia groaned.

"Mrs. Reed is desperate," I said. "She begged the Breens and the Kesebergs to keep her three little ones. They were not happy about it, but took them in."

"Where *is* Reed?" George said.

"We have to assume he's doing the best he can," I said.

I turned back a calendar page, pointing to December 16th. "Twenty-three days now since the snowshoers left," I reminded Elitha and Leanna. "Mr. Stanton knows the way. They're probably resting at Sutter's Fort right now."

"Why don't we walk over, Mother?" Leanna asked.

"I think not," I said.

"We can leave Elitha to take care of Father and the little ones, and you and I and Cousin Solomon and Jean Baptiste can go and bring back help—"

"I'll help Elitha with the babies," Frances piped up from the bed.

I shook my head.

"I'm strong and you're strong," Leanna persisted. "I'm sure we can do it—"

"That's enough," I said, and she went sullenly silent, staring daggers at me.

This morning I went outside, and after not speaking to me since yesterday, Leanna charged out after me. Already an inch taller than I am, she planted herself in front of me and said, "Solomon and Jean Baptiste think we should go too!" When I didn't answer, she burst out, "Father is going to die if we don't get help soon! Don't you understand that?"

Her face was set in defiance, as if she were telling me something I didn't know or daring me to contradict her.

"Oh, Leanna," I said. I reached out for her, and she burst into tears. I held her and said, "Be strong, Leanna. Rescue is coming soon."

When she had calmed, I took her face in my hands. "I'm sure your aunt Elizabeth misses you very much, Leanna. Why don't you go see if you can help her?"

Her eyes narrowed, and she shook her head. "She should not have spoken that way to you, Mother. I cannot forgive her." She turned and went back into our shelter.

I think a lot about walking out. That's why I couldn't lend Mr. Stanton my compass.

Last night, George whispered to me, "Reed and McCutchen would never leave their families here. I think they may have frozen in the snow trying to get here."

I didn't respond directly. That thought has crossed my mind more than once too. "There's still Walter Herron," I said. "And the snowshoers. Don't forget the snowshoers. And if Milt and Margret get through, Milt will come back for us."

"If we'd been there," George said, "Reed wouldn't have been banished."

"Maybe."

"We shouldn't have been two days ahead," he said.

"We went ahead because the grazing was sparse," I said.

"That's true. But the real truth is I just couldn't stand that endless quarreling. I should have been there."

After a moment, I took his hand and whispered, "I wanted to go ahead too."

He squeezed my hand.

Two Days Ahead

"It's good we're pushing ahead," George said. "This way we won't be competing for grazing."

I nodded my head in agreement.

That's what we told each other and ourselves at the time.

October 7th 1846, between Humboldt River and Truckee River

George, Walter Herron, Mr. Reed's teamster riding with us, and I stood outside our wagon on the Trail, waiting for a horseman from the East to catch up with us.

"It's Mr. Reed!" Walter Herron said.

"Hallo, James!" George called. "Come tell us the news."

When James got near we saw his bandaged head, his distress as he dismounted. We gave him as much water as we could spare, and then he began.

We were double-yoking the wagons again to get over another one of those endless sand hills, James said. We had eight wagons already over and five lined up waiting to go.

Graves's first wagon had just pulled over the top of the long, steep hill. You know how hot it was. Everyone was exhausted and drenched with sweat. The men unyoked the extra team of oxen from Graves's first wagon, drove it down the hill, and yoked it to his second wagon, which began the pull up.

Next in line with Graves's third wagon, Graves's teamster, John Snyder, waited for the oxen to be brought back down for him.

Behind Snyder, Milt had already borrowed a yoke and double-teamed our family wagon. "I'm ready, I'm gonna go," Milt said, and he swung out and started to pass Snyder.

Somehow Milt's lead yoke got tangled with Snyder's yoke. "What the Hell——" Snyder began, and then he just exploded and started beating my oxen with his whip.

I rushed up. "Are you crazy, Snyder? Stop beating the oxen!"

His rage switched to me. "You need a good whipping too. You got us into this——"

"Get the wagon over, Snyder," I said. "We'll settle this matter later."

"We'll settle it now," he said, lifting his whip.

"Get the goddamn wagon over, Snyder," I said, and down came his whip butt on my head, blood was pouring in my eyes, he raised his whip again, I drew my knife, Margret rushed up, down came the stroke full upon her, I struck. It all happened in a flash.

Snyder staggered a few steps and fell down dead.

Then everything happened in a blur. I offered boards from my wagon to make a coffin, but Graves would have none of it. Margret was too distraught to bind my wounds, so Virginia had to do it. I should not have asked so much of her. They wrapped Snyder in a shroud, a board below, a board above, and lowered him into the ground. All the women and children were crying. Our family, Milt Elliott, and the Eddys stood on one side. The Graves family, the Kesebergs, the Wolfingers, Reinhardt, Spitzer, and the Murphy clan stood on the other. The nine Breens stood apart from either group.

All of a sudden, Graves pointed to me. "You murdered John Snyder!"

"It was self-defense——" Milt began.

Keseberg cut him off. "An eye for an eye! Hang him!"

I bared my neck. "Come ahead, gentlemen."

No one moved.

*Graves and the larger group moved away to confer while Milt, William
Eddy, and I drew our weapons and stood ready.*

Graves stepped forward. "Banishment. On foot. No weapons."

"You're sending him out to die!" Eddy said.

"I refuse to leave," I said.

Graves drew his gun.

"They'll kill you," Margret sobbed. "I beg you to go."

"Never."

Graves cocked his pistol.

I cocked mine.

"We can't afford any more bad blood here," Graves said.

"Go and bring us back food," Margret begged.

*I looked from Margret to Graves. "I will go if you promise to take care
of my family."*

Graves made a small nod.

*He took my gun, I said Good-bye to my family, and started out alone
on foot, listening to the sobs behind me.*

*That night, I heard horses galloping in the dark and thought they were
coming to kill me. I hid myself, ready to fight until their death or mine. It
was Virginia and Milt bringing me a horse, a gun, and some food.*

George and I were shocked almost speechless.

John Snyder dead?

James Reed banished?

"How could this happen?" I finally got out.

James just looked baffled, stunned.

"You can't go out alone, James," George said. "Our horses are
gone, but . . ." George looked at Walter Herron. Walter looked
uncertainly at the horizon.

George took him aside.

"Mr. Donner, I don't want to go out there," Walter Herron said.

"For a man alone, it's a death sentence," George said. "Two men have a chance." And after a moment, "You're his teamster, Walter." And another moment, "There's nobody else."

James Reed and Walter Herron, sharing one horse, rode west.

Jan 11th 1847

The swelling and inflammation has spread above George's wrist. He's in evident pain, but never mentions it. I cleanse the wound daily with warm compresses, which seem to comfort him.

I forgot to write down about Elitha's smoking the other day. When I had finished bathing George's wound, I fixed a pipe for him, tamped down the tobacco, lit it, drew deeply, and handed it to him.

"Where did you learn to do that?" he asked.

"I used to do it for my father," I said. "I love the smell of pipe tobacco."

"Your mother never fails to amaze me," George said to the children. He smoked his pipe and watched me write a new name.

DEATHS IN THE MOUNTAINS

Baylis Williams 25, d. Dec 15th 1846 at the lake camp. From Springfield, the Reeds' handyman, brother of Lizzie Williams.

Jacob Donner, 58, d. Dec 16th 1846 at Alder Creek. Born in North Carolina, recently of Springfield, Illinois, beloved husband, father, brother.

Samuel Shoemaker, 25, d. Dec 17th 1846 at Alder Creek. Donner teamster from Springfield. Calf-lifting champion.

James Smith, 25, d. Dec 20th 1846 at Alder Creek. Reed teamster from Springfield.

Joseph Reinhardt, 30?, d. Dec 20th 1846 at Alder Creek. From
Germany, partner with Augustus Spitzer?

Charles Burger, 30?, d. Dec 29th 1846 at the lake camp. Donner
teamster.

"Dutch Charley," George said. "He was a good teamster. He
respected the animals and they responded in kind."

I nodded, closed the Bible, and spread out the calendar. "Your
turn to mark the date today, Elitha."

Elitha lay listlessly on the platform. She has stopped reading.
"Elitha," I repeated.

"Someone else can have it," she said.

"No, it's your turn. I don't want to get it all mixed up." I
waited until she finally came to the table, then I said, "George,
give Elitha a little puff."

George looked at me in surprise. When I nodded, he said,
"Knock me over with a feather." He handed the pipe to Elitha,
who was also surprised and perked up almost instantly. "Now
don't draw too deeply, Elitha," George said, "or it'll make you
cough."

All her sisters watched Elitha closely as she drew too deeply
and coughed. The second time she drew more shallowly without
coughing and looked pleased with herself.

"Now can I have a puff?" Leanna said.

"You're too young," I said. "That's enough, Elitha. Give the
pipe back to your father and mark the day."

After Elitha had marked the big red *X* on January 8, I pointed
back to January 4 and said, "Jean Baptiste said that Margret and
Virginia Reed, Milt Elliott, and their cook, Lizzie, set out here
to cross the mountains on foot."

I've thought of them constantly in the last seven days, Godspeed,
Milt and Margret. They may already have reached the valley.

That night on our platform, George asked, "Why did you let Elitha smoke?"

"She's barely able to stomach the hides," I said. "She tries, but they make her nauseated. Tobacco takes the edge off the appetite."

He lay there thinking, then asked, "Is that why you started smoking?"

I pretended to be asleep. He moved close to me and spooned his body about mine. His legs are so long that the first time he did that, shortly after we were married, I said, "You're more than a spoon. You're a whole cutlery set." He thought that was the funniest thing imaginable. Now he whispered in my ear, "More than a spoon." Even though I was supposed to be asleep, I moved into the curve of his body.

Jan 12th 1847

I was too upset to write last night.

We heard a noise outside, and it was Milt and the Reeds' cook, Lizzie. It was a terrible disappointment to see them. I could barely hide it as I led them to the fire and fixed them a cup of hot water.

"Lizzie gave out the first day and went back," Milt said.

"Oh, Mrs. Donner, it was terrible," Lizzie said. "The wild beasts howled . . ." She started howling herself.

"On the fifth day Virginia's feet froze and we turned back," Milt said. "When I couldn't carry Virginia anymore, Mrs. Reed and I dragged her. Then she crawled. Thank God we came back. The storm that night would have killed us. The Breens took in Mrs. Reed and the children." He looked from George to me, then back to George, and said, "I'm sorry, Uncle George."

Milt is 28 and very strong, but George says that even as a boy he was all limbs, and he has never outgrown that touching gangliness. His hands were red and mottled on the cup of hot water, and I stopped thinking of my own disappointment and started thinking of his.

"Please don't make me eat hides, Mrs. Donner," Lizzie said. "Mrs. Reed told me to live or die on them. I can't stomach hides, I can't . . ." She started wailing again.

I looked at her, Betsey, and all I could see was a fleshy version of her standing outside the Reed family wagon, pouring a cascade of luscious wild blackberries onto huge, steaming golden biscuits, ladling mounds of fresh cream on top . . .

"Please, Mrs. Donner," she begged. "Just give me a bit of meat."

"If we had meat, we would be eating it, Lizzie," I said. "I wish to God we had more hides."

She slept on a hide by the fire and fretted all night long.

This morning, I was braiding Eliza's hair and keeping my eye on Lizzie, perched uneasily on a stool, wringing her hands.

Elitha, who never misses her daily tobacco puffs, was telling a Bible story to Frances and Georgia. "And when Daniel was taken out of the den of lions, not one mark was found on him . . ."

On his platform, George, wrapped in blankets, talked intently to Milt. I heard him say, "Jean Baptiste and I figure we can relay the children . . ."

Leanna, who considers Elitha's smoking disgusting, unless she can have a puff too, was shaking out bedding. Through a gap in her blanket, I saw Mrs. Wolfinger lying perfectly still on her rack, her little, gulping sobs constant as ever.

"Not one mark at all, because Daniel had trusted in his God. Then the king rounded up all the wicked people"—suddenly Elitha burst out—"who had *done* this to Daniel like Lansford Hastings and cast *them* into the lions' den, and they did not even reach the bottom before the lions fell upon them and crushed all their bones to pieces—"

"The important part, Elitha," I said, "is that Daniel lay down with the lions and rose up unharmed. And he did that with the help of God. Just as we are."

Suddenly Lizzie cried, "God has cursed us for leaving that old man on the trail. We're all gonna die. We're cursed, cur—"

I flew across the room, seeing the children's scared, shocked faces before I grabbed Lizzie, her cries cutting off abruptly, her face stunned as I propelled her to the stairs and turned to Milt. "Milt, you and Jean Baptiste take Lizzie back to the lake camp now."

After they left, I finished Eliza's hair, Elitha finished her story, and Frances, Georgia, and Eliza went to their platform to play their card game. An hour later, Frances shuffled the cards, dealt them out, looked over at me, and asked, "Is that true what Lizzie said, Mother?" Her tone was matter-of-fact, so accepting it pierced my heart.

"No, Frances," I said. "God doesn't curse people. People do that to themselves."

Hardcoop Left Behind

The nearly impenetrable Wasatch Mountains and the Great Salt Lake Desert behind us, John Snyder dead, James Reed banished, he and Walter Herron specks on the horizon, and then the specks too gone, we waited in dismay and agitation for the rest of the company to catch up with us. George, very much the Captain then, looked sternly around the campfire at the tense, defensive faces. "Reed said it was self-defense—"

"It was, Uncle George—" Milt began.

"It was murder," Graves said, "and we were lenient."

"Snyder attacked him—" George began.

"You weren't there, Donner."

I searched the crowd again, interrupting the chorus of arguments. "Where's Hardcoop?"

The faces turned guilty, eyes averted, except for William Eddy, who said, "Ask Keseberg. Or Breen or Graves."

When no one volunteered more, I looked questioningly at Margret Reed.

"Everyone had to walk to spare the oxen," Margret said. "James was gone. We abandoned our last wagon. Everything. Even Mother's rocking chair that Father made. She nursed all my brothers and me in it, I nursed all my children—" Margret started crying.

"Margret, gather yourself and tell us where Hardcoop is."

But she kept crying and looking at the ground.

Finally Lewis Keseberg said, "He couldn't keep up."

And this is the story they told us in blurts, sobs, defiance, and defense. We could easily picture it.

A rocking chair sits in the sun. Margret Reed and her children cry as they walk away from their big family wagon that Sarah Keyes died in.

Ahead in the line, Keseberg finds the old Belgian Hardcoop hiding inside his wagon and angrily pulls him out.

"I won't be able to keep up," Hardcoop says.

"Everyone must walk," Keseberg says.

Hardcoop, crying, goes to William Eddy, who's helping with Graves's third wagon. "Please let me ride," he says.

"Wait'll we get over this sandy stretch," Eddy says, "and I'll see what I can do."

The sand sifts around the wheel rims. The men grasp the rear wheel spokes and try to wrestle the wagon forward. It doesn't budge. Sweaty silt pours into their red, burning eyes, as they heave again.

Again.

And again, until it finally moves.

Then they start on the next wagon.

At the campfire that night, Eddy suddenly jumps up and says, "Where's Hardcoop?"

Antonio, the Mexican herder, says, "He was sitting in the road when I came by with the cattle."

Eddy and Milt Elliott, who share the night watch, build a large fire on the side of a hill, stoke it all night long, hoping that somewhere in the darkness Hardcoop will see it and take direction and heart.

At dawn, Eddy goes to Lewis Keseberg. "Hardcoop never came in. I'll go with you to get him."

"Go back?" Keseberg says. "Are you crazy?"

Eddy goes to Graves. "Lend me your horse to get Hardcoop."

Graves shakes his head no.

Breen stands nearby with no already on his face. "Use your wits, Eddy,"
Breen says. "We can't risk our horses to lug in a dead man."
The wagons roll on.

George managed to speak first. "Why didn't any of you help
Eddy?"

"What's wrong with you?" I said.

Margret Reed and Philippine Keseberg wept. Most looked
furtive and ashamed. Only Mr. Keseberg looked steadily at me.

Inside our wagon, I opened the Bible the missionary gave us
in Independence "for the heathens."

DEATHS ON THE TRAIL

Underneath

Sarah Keyes, 70, d. May 26th 1846 at Alcove Springs, Kansas.
Margret Reed's mother. Peacefully of old age, her daugh-
ter, son-in-law, and grandchildren around her.
Luke Halloran, 25, d. Aug 25th 1846 on the south side of Salt
Lake, of tuberculosis, traveling in our wagon from Little
Sandy, the "Parting of the Ways."
John Snyder, 25, d. Oct. 5th 1846 in Nevada territory. Franklin
Graves's teamster, "Driver par Excellence," accidentally
killed by James Reed.

I wrote,

Hardcoop, 60?, d. Oct

I stopped writing and looked up. "I don't even know what date
to put. How long did it take him to die?" When George didn't

answer, I said, "We don't know these people at all. Even Margret Reed is not herself. George! We're starting a new country and already it's tainted."

George shook his head, as if still in disbelief. "We weren't there, Tamsen. None of us knows what we'll do until we're tested."

"I know I wouldn't leave somebody to die alone if I could help it!"

We went to bed in silence. No matter how tightly I closed my eyes, all I could see was the same debased image: an old man crawling toward disappearing wagons.

Hardcoop, 60?, d. Oct 7–8th? 1846 in the desert. Originally from Belgium, one daughter there, name unknown. Abandoned.

What I Know About Hardcoop

*P*erhaps the daughter someplace in Belgium will go to her grave wondering what happened to her father, or she may have stopped thinking about him long ago. Even if I knew her address, I could not tell her much.

He joined us in Independence, Missouri. I never heard his given name and never thought to ask. He was always called Hardcoop, never Mr. Hardcoop. From the beginning, everyone thought of him as an old man. Frances, Georgia, and Eliza called him Grandpa, as they have been taught to call aged people.

He was from Belgium, having one last adventure before going back home to live with his daughter. (Had he told her this plan? Did she prepare? Does she wait?)

He had been in the US for many years, had worked as a cooper—on the Trail he repaired our wooden water cask better than new. I thought later that maybe Hardcoop was only a nickname and not his real name at all.

He spoke English with a heavy accent; he and Mr. Keseberg conversed in German, Hardcoop told me the day he fixed our cask. "We don't converse much," he said drily. Then, though he was hardly taller than I, Hardcoop stood like a Prussian soldier, making me laugh as he imitated Mr. Keseberg: "I know German, French, and English, and I will soon know Spanish. I do not nor will I ever speak Flemish, which is a ridiculous language, and it hurts my ears the way you massacre English. We shall speak in German if we need to speak."

Even I thought of Hardcoop as an old man, though he and George were nearly the same age.

He weakened fast in the Wasatch. One day when the men were wrestling with a huge boulder, he nearly pitched over. "Bumbler!" snarled a teamster a third his age. Ashamed, Hardcoop approached me. "I need to rest a little," he said. "I can watch the children."

"Can you sit with Mr. Halloran?" I asked. "He's not well."

For two days, Hardcoop sat with Luke and cared for the young man as tenderly as ever I could. He said he had twin grandsons Luke's age that he hadn't seen since they were little boys. "I will be glad to see them," he said. "I hope they'll be glad to see me——"

"Hardcoop! Get out here!" angry voices called from outside our wagon. "You too, Halloran."

I wrenched the curtain back. "Go away," I said to the fuming men.

"We've made six miles in five days! *Get out here now, shirkers, or we'll drag you out!*"

Luke Halloran, deathly pale, and Hardcoop, red with shame, climbed down.

Lewis Keseberg stared steadily back at me, unashamed.

William Eddy said that since Hardcoop had paid Keseberg to ride with him, Keseberg had a particular responsibility. Well, didn't he? The others too! Hardcoop was a member of the Party!

The Party.

"We shouldn't have gone ahead," George said again last night. "I'm the Captain. I should have been with the company."

"Were we still a company?" I asked. He didn't answer.

I've lived years on farms, and know incontestably that the strong survive, the weak die off. That is the way of nature, but

I used to argue that we can improve on nature, or at least not be as brutal as nature. I don't have the luxury of theoretical debates anymore, nor am I as sentimental as I once was. Although I want to believe I would have gone back for Hardcoop, I realize now that Mr. Keseberg knew his first imperative was to save himself and his family before a sickly paying passenger, and he was the only one of us to baldly admit it.

My dearest only sister,

Jean Baptiste came into camp empty-handed and discouraged again, and it took me some time to buck him up. He just left, everyone else is finally asleep, and again I can think what I want and write what I please. I ran out of writing paper some time ago and began writing you here in my journal. I think I am always talking to you anyway. It helps me sort out the muddle in my head. What would Betsey Poor do, I ask myself, and see you standing there in your snug clapboard in Newburyport, calm, unshaken, in the midst of your hectic family life. You were as much a mother to me as a sister after our dearest mother in the world departed from us, and your wise counsel guided me again after our dear stepmother died. I often speak of Aunty Poor to my daughters, and they know you and my niece and nephews as if they had seen you many times. "Ask Aunty Poor if little Will's ear is better," one or the other will say or "Tell Aunty Poor to bring her Elizabeth here to play with me." It is my dearest hope that they and I will see you, Mr. Poor, and your dear babes in person this side of the vale.

Will you ever read the pile of letters I have already written you or this journal? Will you ever know how I long for you to be here with me?

Were you here, dear sister, hopes would be doubled, burdens halved.

My beloved husband grows weaker each day. We do not speak of it, nor have we ever spoken about the accident on my 45th birthday, when our wagon tipped over.

There is much we do not speak of, Betsey. Fear lies so close to the surface it cannot be fanned.

I am fortunate in that I have always been able to hide my feelings successfully.

Tonight I want to tell you about my sister-in-law, Elizabeth. She and I have never had an intimacy like ours, but we are close in age, and married to brothers. Those things were sufficient to forge a bond, I thought, even though Elizabeth was more interested in cooking than I am in books. "Guess what I cooked today" is how she greeted me daily for seven years. But Elizabeth is far superior to me in patience, a saint really. I could never have lived a second with her husband, Jacob, a complaining, whining man from the day I met him. George used to describe a Jacob so robust in body and spirit that, until this trip, when Jacob blossomed before my eyes, I wondered if it were just something he wanted to believe about his brother. I must admit that I've also most unkindly wondered if Elizabeth's extraordinary patience with Jacob was just gratitude for his presence.

Elizabeth's first husband, James Hook, and father of her two oldest sons, Solomon and William, abandoned the family in 1834. As modern as Springfield felt itself to be, it was still frontier, an arduous place for a woman alone with a farm to run and two little boys to raise. Elizabeth filed a suit for divorce, and George, who married her sister, Mary Blue, in a double wedding the same day Elizabeth married James Hook, testified on her behalf. Elizabeth married Jacob in 1835. All of this happened before I came to Springfield, but of course, in a small town you soon hear everything. Elizabeth and I have never spoken about her divorce, but I have always tried to convey that my sympathies are entirely with her. George says that, before Elizabeth married James Hook, she was "lively and gay." And Leanna says that sometimes, when they cook together, Elizabeth laughs. I have never been privileged to see that side of her. Although usually amiable to me, she holds herself private, and there is a brittleness about her. Who can blame her?

I'm sure I wrote you about all the months that Elizabeth and I prepared together for the trip. But maybe I didn't, and either way, it helps me pass the hours. More important, I find that, when I revisit the past, it often reveals something quite unexpected—too often some humbling or unpleasant truth that seems clear as day now. Those were joyful months of anticipation for me, and for Elizabeth too, I thought. Almost every day on our way back from town, George and I never passed their farmhouse to go on to ours without stopping to show the mail-order packages that had just arrived.

My arms loaded with parcels, Elitha, Leanna, Frances, and Georgia on my heels, I pushed open their kitchen door, "Elizabeth!" George had Eliza astride his shoulders and an armload of bolts of silks, satins, laces, and velvets.

Our niece Mary and four of our six nephews accosted us with noise and hugs. "Aunt Tamsen! Uncle George!"

"Aunt Elizabeth," Leanna said, pecking her aunt's cheek at the oven and immediately donning apron and pot holders to help her.

"Look what came!" I said.

"Just the first load," George said. "I'll be meeting myself coming and going to town all day long."

"Guess what I cooked today," Elizabeth said, handing Leanna steaming pies to put on cooling racks. "Blueberry pies. At this time of year!"

I tore open the first mail-order parcel, filled with bright blue and red calico handkerchiefs, glass beads, brass finger rings, spyglasses . . . "Peace offerings for the Indians," I said.

A little chill passed through the room, and Elizabeth's eyes shot to mine. Indians were one of the Trail's biggest fears.

"Oh, aren't you afraid, Mrs. Donner?" Effie, the hired girl, said.

"Mother's not afraid of anything," Leanna said, but Effie, eyes wide, continued. "The savages kidnap white women, pass them around . . ."

"Hush, Effie," I said. "You read too many penny novels." Quickly I opened a second parcel addressed to T. E. Donner: filled with watercolors, oil paints, rulers . . .

"More school supplies," George said. "Now what is that?"

"That's apparatus for preserving botanical specimens," I said.

George turned to the children. "Your mother came into my cornfield looking for specimens. And I'm the specimen she found."

Elitha and Leanna rolled their eyes good-naturedly: they'd heard this joke before.

I pointed to a box. "Open that one, George."

Inside the big box was a pair of gleaming leather boots. George beamed.

"Handmade in Boston," I said. "Size twelve and a half. If we have to ford any creeks, we can ride in them."

Of course George had to put on his new boots right then. His childlike pleasure gave me pleasure. With the children taking turns riding on his feet, he strode around the room in his new boots. "Wait'll Jacob sees these," he said.

"He's out in the barn with the teamsters," Elizabeth said. "Wait." She handed George a half a pie.

George took a big bite and declared, "Elizabeth, you are the best cook in the world. Except for my wife, of course."

"I set a good table," I said, "but it pales next to Elizabeth's."

Elizabeth beamed and said, "And my apprentice is going to rival me." Leanna beamed, and George left, trailed by a pack of nephews.

"We're taking ten pounds of sugar apiece," Elizabeth said.

"Take twenty," I said.

"Twenty apiece? We'll have enough to feed an army. I could make pies every day. Well, I hope you think ten pounds of salt apiece will be enough. *Children, keep the ruckus down! Who wants to take pies out to the barn?"*

Leanna was whipping cream for the pies, Elitha already immersed in one of the new books. The other children, in happy chaos, adorned themselves with rings and bracelets. "When I finish this, bet I can get more bracelets on my arm than you," Leanna said to her cousin Mary, who had bracelets up to her elbow. Frances peered at them all through a spyglass.

"I will," I said, taking the two pies from Elizabeth—

Georgia is whimpering, I must stop.

Betsey,

I need to tell you what happened after Jacob died.

December 18th 1846

In the clearing, wind and snow swirling around us, George, Leanna, Elizabeth, her older children, Jean Baptiste, Milt Elliott, and I hastily buried Jacob, wrapped in a quilt, in the snow.

George's eyes were full of tears. "He'd still be alive if I hadn't talked him into this. He didn't want to go. He didn't even want—"

I put my arm around him. "Your brother had the greatest adventure of his life."

Elizabeth whirled around. "You both told Jacob he'd live out his days in a warm place. We should never have listened to you." She looked at me with fury. "What were you thinking? You're a mother. You should have known better. We're all going to die."

Leanna was so shocked she dropped her aunt's hand, and the remark cut me so much I knew there had to be truth in it.

I try not to think about them, but her words burn inside me. Leanna has refused to go to Elizabeth's shelter since that day, nor will she talk about it.

How I wish you were here to give me counsel and comfort.

Your sister

Jan 15th, 75 days in the mountains

I just realized with almost incredulity, Betsey, that you know nothing about these things indelibly seared in my mind.

I know not if my earlier letters wended their way to you, but think some must have. I wrote you and Allen Francis at least a half dozen times on the Trail, once enclosing prairie flower seeds I had dried for you.

I never wrote anyone after we swung southwest from Fort Bridger to take Hastings Cutoff—not that we ever saw an eastbound rider to give letters to. Even if my hands had been free, our minds and hearts were filled with anxiety. I recorded the dead in the Bible. I wrote only sporadically in my journal. Now my pen must do double duty: the particulars for you, dearest sister, the record for the book I planned to publish.

George and I go over it all endlessly. In our heads, at the fire, on our platforms at night. At first I asked him not to ruminate in front of the children, but then he went so many miles away from all of us that I couldn't bear watching him suffering alone in his head. We talk through every step, but we always dead-end, never can find the certain mistake that brought us here. Fortunately, the little ones show no interest. In the beginning, Elitha and Leanna whispered together after their sisters fell asleep, but now Elitha claps her hands over her ears and goes under her blanket. More than once Leanna has said in exasperation, "What does it matter? We can't go back and do it over."

What does it matter indeed. Even if we found an answer

where we could look at each other and say, Yes, yes, *that* was it, it's not a way out of here. Yet we remain consumed.

I am lucky to have the habit and solace and quiet of writing. Sometimes I too want to clap my hands over my ears when George says one more time as if for the first time, If we hadn't taken Hastings Cutoff . . . If we hadn't spent a whole day for Luke Halloran's burial . . . If we hadn't spent three days in Truckee Meadows . . . If, if, if . . .

The other day, George said, "You were right about Hastings Cutoff. I should have listened to you."

There was a time I might have snapped, Yes, you should have. But what good would that do any of us now? That I was right is bitter comfort.

Still, I must admit, dear sister, and it will not surprise you, anger flashed through me.

Sept 21st 1846

Dear Allen,

I know not if my other letters have reached you, but think surely some have. I wrote you and my sister, Betsey, at least a half dozen times on the Trail, the letters piling up until a horseman coming from the West heading back East was kind enough to carry them with him. I gave three letters to the mountain man James Clyman at Fort Laramie in early July the morning he left. He put them carefully in his pack, leaned down from his horse, and said, "Lansford Hastings has more ambition than sense, Mrs. Donner. Talk to your husband."

We put our lives into the hands of a false prophet, Allen. He was gone when we arrived at Fort Bridger, the man who promised us guidance on the short, high road to California gone a week already, but off we went, everyone but me in a general rush of good spirits, to catch up with the elusive Hastings. "Where others have gone, we can follow," they shouted.

But only one wagon train had gone before us, and soon we were forced to leave even those faint tracks and make a new road through the tortuous Wasatch Mountains. We have had bickering from the beginning, but the Wasatch was where—

. . .

Jan 16th 1847

Betsey, this wrinkled and soiled paper is a letter I began to Allen Francis last September, warning future emigrants not to take Hastings Cutoff. I know not what interrupted me or why I stuck it in the Bible, but there it remained until I found it just now along with a letter just begun to you. I can only hope that James Reed at Sutter's Fort has sent a warning letter back to Springfield.

Hastings Cutoff

*A*t almost every campfire, Betsey, one man or another brought out that little red book James Reed waved so enthusiastically in our farmhouse that long ago winter's evening—"Hastings discovered a shortcut!"—and debated whether to take Hastings Cutoff.

At Fort Laramie, in early July, the mountain man James Clyman, heading east, galloped up to the Reed wagons and shouted, "Where is the noble James Reed who served in the Black Hawk War with Abraham Lincoln and James Clyman?"

Reed greeted him with a big smile and a bear hug, then drew back. "Clyman, you still don't bathe."

At the campfire that night, Mr. Clyman said, "Don't take the Cutoff. I've ridden with Hastings. He's no mountain man."

"With all due respect, Jim, this is 1846," James said. "The days of the mountain men are over."

Mr. Clyman shook his head and said, "Reed, you still don't listen."

A week later, a horseman from the West rode down our entire line of wagons, calling out a message from Hastings himself: "I wait at Fort Bridger to personally lead your wagons over my Cutoff."

I turned to George. "Mr. Clyman said you can't take wagons through that wilderness. He's ridden that country."

"With Hastings to lead us, what could go wrong?" George said.

July 19th, 1846, at Little Sandy, we reached the campfire of decision. We would either continue on the regular Fort Hall road or swing southwest to Fort Bridger to take the new short-cut. I had a very bad feeling. It was late, the men were tense, they had been arguing for hours.

"You can't ignore that the Stevens Party of '44 barely got through on the regular route——" the Irishman Patrick Breen said.

James Reed cut him off. "If I have to hear about the Stevens Party one more time, Breen——"

"What about the dry run?" the German Lewis Keseberg said again. "We already have to get women and children across one desert."

James Reed looked at Mr. Keseberg with uncontrolled disdain. "At worst, it's only forty miles. Men who fear forty miles belong back East."

James didn't see the look of hatred Mr. Keseberg directed at him, though it was clear enough to me ten feet away. With a stick, he retraced the Cutoff across the base of the rough triangle of Hastings Cutoff drawn in the dirt in front of him. "It's clear as day," he said again. "We cut across the base here——"

"I think we should take it," Luke Halloran, a slight, rosy-cheeked young Irishman from Missouri, said again.

I cleared my throat. George didn't look over at me, but he said, "Remember what Jim Clyman said, 'Take the established route and never leave it——'"

Ignoring George, James said, "Lansford Hastings himself waits at Fort Bridger to lead us."

George persisted. "Clyman said Hastings doesn't know what he's talking about."

"For God's sake, George, there's a nearer route," James said. "There's no reason to take such a roundabout course."

"I'm not necessarily against taking the Cutoff," Mr. Breen said, "but

we should remember one of the Stevens Party of '44 had to stay all winter in the mountains—"

"Call the vote," James said.

I cleared my throat again, and then coughed, but George said nothing. He looked as if he were in an agony of indecision. "Mr. Donner," I said.

A couple of the teamsters snickered; Reed's eyebrows shot up; George remained silent.

"Call the vote," James repeated.

"Those in favor of taking Hastings Cutoff say Aye," Mr. Halloran said.

"Aye!" James Reed shouted.

"My wife will set down the names," George said, the first acknowledgment of my presence, though all the men knew I had been there all night, as I often am there sitting on my little campstool outside the ring of men, writing in my journal balanced on my lap. So upset I could barely write, I started recording the vote.

"James Reed. Aye!"

"Luke Halloran. Aye!"

"Patrick Breen from the Auld Sod, now a proud citizen of America, lately of Keokuk, Iowa—"

"Get on with it, Breen," Reed said.

Breen's brogue continued unrushed. "—soon to be a child of California, God's own country itself. Patrick Breen. Aye."

Mr. Eddy answered without hesitation. "William Eddy. Aye!"

"Lewis Keseberg. Aye."

"Hardcoop. One last adventure, and then it's home to Belgium to live with my daughter. Aye!"

George was next in the circle. He looked at the map drawn in the dirt. Looked at the mountain, its top covered with snow. Looked back at the map. Looked everyplace except at me.

"Judas Priest, George, piss or get off the pot," James said.

"George Donner," he said. And, after an interminable pause, "Aye."

I jumped up, words bursting out of me. "How can you even think of leaving the old road and entrusting our lives to a man we know nothing about?"

All the men went silent. George half stood, then sat back down, looked at the ground. I left noisily, hearing the silence behind me.

James Reed broke the silence, "Stanton, you set down the rest of the names."

"Jacob Donner," I heard and turned around. Jacob looked at George, but George still looked down.

Jacob mumbled something.

"Was that an Aye, Jacob?" Reed said.

Jacob nodded his head. Yes.

"Charles Stanton. Well, I'm riding with George Donner, so it's an Aye for me."

Reed, jubilant, uncorked whiskey.

Inside the wagon, I got into bed, fully dressed, my heart pounding, Mr. Clyman's words pounding, Take the established route and never leave it. It's barely possible to get through before the snows if you follow it, and it may be impossible if you don't.

An hour later, George climbed under the blanket and reached out for me. I pulled away.

"I'm the one who should be upset," he said. "You embarrassed me."

I sat up, livid. "You were embarrassed? You should have been ashamed. James Reed just bullied this through. And you went along with him."

"Sometimes you go too far—" George began.

"Too far? And may I ask who is setting the boundaries, Mr. Donner?"

"Tamsen, you know I thought about the Cutoff a long time—"

"It didn't need thinking about. And Jacob just went along with you. It's wrong that women aren't allowed at the campfire, it's immoral. If we had a vote, there's no way it would've passed—"

"They elected me Captain——"

"Captain? All the Captain does is select campsites and set the morning departure time. Did you endanger us all just to be Captain? Do you always have to be so agreeable? I can't understand how you——"

George's voice was cold. "It's done now. From now on, we'll be known as the Donner Party."

I was so upset I couldn't sleep, Betsey. George was awake too, he tossed and turned.

I lay still as a rock.

The perfidy. How could he? Just that morning, at our campfire, we had been in agreement . . .

"I'm leaning toward taking the shortcut," George said.

"After what Mr. Clyman said?"

He looked at the Weber Mountain peaks, capped with snow. "July nineteenth, and look at those peaks. I thought I knew all kinds of country. I've seen drought, locusts, even a tornado, but I don't understand this strange land at all."

"That's why we should take the established route."

After a moment, he nodded. "I guess you're right. I just want us to get to California the fastest we can. I don't feel comfortable with this weather."

Yes, I'm right, I raged inside, and it's *wrong* that the women don't have a vote, he knows that.

I knew if I spoke, I would say ugly things.

I lay there angry and afraid.

Jan 18th 1847

*W*hen I think about Lansford Hastings now, I feel almost de-tached, someplace in these terrible months his shoulders grown too weak to bear full responsibility for this nightmare.

We prepared carefully. That is some consolation to us. Information about '44 was widely available, and the great successes of '45 continued to filter back. Scarcely a week went by in our months of planning without another newspaper dispatch come directly from the new country, and I would be surprised if more than a half dozen of the scores of letters scribbled by those already en route escaped our eager eyes. Allen Francis brought each letter to our reading circle before he even published them in the paper.

Our eagerness was always tempered with prudence, because we of '46 were the first families on the Trail.

It's strange, Betsey. Things I hardly thought about in the rush of those days come back now, the smallest detail etched clearly, as if it had been stowed somewhere carelessly in haste to emerge slowly and completely in confinement.

February 1846 Illinois

Outside our window, it was snowing heavily. Inside our cozy farmhouse, George piled more wood on the fire, and set the chairs in a semicircle around the hearth. Allen Francis and I were looking through a new book, I can feel the heft of it in my hands this second. My sister-in-law, Elizabeth, Elitha, and Leanna put refreshments on the table. They were using my good rose-patterned china. George's brother, Jacob, was half dozing in an easy chair, as usual.

"What will you read this week, Mother?" Elitha asked.

I held up the book, and read its title, "*Report of the Exploring Expedition to the Rocky Mountains in the Year 1842, and to Oregon and North California in the Years 1843–44* by John Frémont."

She wrinkled up her nose.

"This is history in the making, Elitha."

"I'd rather Dickens," she said.

Jacob glanced up. "I'd rather my feather bed."

"We might fight Indians, Uncle Jacob—" Leanna began excitedly.

But Jacob had already sunk back, his mouth gaping open. I wanted to shake him, but I concealed my annoyance and said, "Let's hope not, Leanna. We'll wait a few minutes more for Mr. and Mrs. Reed—"

I didn't see Frances in her nightgown tiptoe to the table, reach for a small cake, and knock off the china cup, but I heard it hit the floor and break.

"Frances!"

Now I see her face crumple, but then, I knelt down, picked up the cup and its broken handle, looked at it with distress.

"You know you're never supposed to touch my china, Frances. That's all I have from my mother . . ."

Frances started to cry.

"Crying isn't going to fix it, Frances," I said. "Don't touch my china again."

I might have gone on haranguing her, but the door burst open with a *whoosh* of wind and snow. James Reed waved a book and shouted, "Hastings discovered a shortcut!"

Behind James, Margret tried in vain to restrain him. "James, your boots. The floor——"

"No one worries about snow in California, Mrs. Reed," I said.

"Hot off the presses!" James said. "We can save three hundred miles!"

Then everyone gathered round him, talking at once. In all the hubbub, Georgia and Eliza ran out in their nightgowns and yelled happily with everyone else. Even Jacob perked up.

Jan 19th 1847

Today was the fourth day we were unable to go outside. Elitha, Leanna, and Frances were huddled by the fireplace, drinking cups of hot water, which I used to call "tea," until the day Leanna shouted, "It's only water! Call it water!" I was polishing George's boots with an ointment we use for oxen udders. Rub and polish, my hand moved methodically, firelight flickering over his trail-worn boots . . .

"Again!" Eliza shrieked. "Hold on tight," George said, and grinning at me, he took giant steps around Elizabeth's kitchen in his gleaming new boots, Eliza on one foot, Georgia on the other, squealing in delight.

I looked up from the scarred and grooved boot in my hand. George was propped up on his platform, Georgia and Eliza lying listlessly under a blanket next to him. "Your turn for the lesson, George," I said.

"I was born in North Carolina of . . . ," George began. His tone was flat, almost rote. His spirits fluctuate as often as mine.

"Did you know Mother there?" Frances asked.

A little laugh burst out of me, and it was so unexpected, such a rare sound in the shelter, that it startled us all and completely changed the atmosphere. When George began again, it was in his old voice. Even after all his years of traveling, he has never lost his soft and easy North Carolina accent. "You carry a perfect Southern day in your words," I told him soon after we met. I didn't say that more than one woman has been led astray by a man's voice.

How curious that I married two men from North Carolina, two men whose voices could charm larks from the trees. Tully and George were alike in other ways too, I was thinking . . .

"This is a few years before your mother was on this earth, Frances," George said. "Now I was saying. I was born in North Carolina of Revolutionary stock—"

"I'm Revolutionary stock too," I said. "My father, your grandfather Eustis, enlisted when the Revolutionary War began. He was 15. A sentinel at Old North in Boston, Massachusetts, the same place that gave the warning that the British were coming."

"One if by land, two if by sea," Frances said.

"You're Revolutionary stock on both sides, children," George said. "You can always be proud of that."

It's a fierce pride George and I have always shared. "Americans bow to no master," I said.

George nodded and went on. "When I was 18, your uncle Jacob and I went to the land of Daniel Boone. Where is that, Elitha?"

"Kentucky," Elitha said.

"On to Indiana," George said.

"Then to Illinois," Elitha and Leanna said simultaneously with George.

And after a tiny pause, the three of them said again simultaneously, "To Texas. All of us together." They smiled at each other. It was almost playful.

"Back to Illinois again," George said. "I buried two wives there, including Elitha and Leanna's mother, Mary Blue."

Elitha spoke next and with some importance. "Our mother, Mary Blue, and her sister, Elizabeth Blue, married Father and Uncle Jacob. Two sisters married two brothers."

"Aunt Elizabeth is our double aunt, and Uncle Jacob was our double uncle," Leanna said.

"Why doesn't Aunt Elizabeth ever come here?" Frances asked.

"What were you thinking?" I wrenched my mind away from Elizabeth's words back to the boots and Leanna's voice. "She's busy with our double cousins," Leanna said.

"If any of you ever decide to go back to Illinois," George said, "you have family there who will help you. You have your half brother, George. You have your five half sisters . . ."

Springfield, Illinois, 1839

George, 53, and I, 38, strolled a bit ahead of Elitha, 6, and Leanna, 5, dragging sticks in the dirt road behind us. George gestured to them.

"Except for Elitha and Leanna," he said, "my son and other five daughters are all on their own——"

I looked up at him in astonishment. "You have eight children?"

With a twinkle he said, "So far."

"I understand you've recently returned from Texas, Mr. Donner," I said. "You didn't find it to your liking?"

"We put in one crop," George said. "My brother and sister-in-law didn't like Texas from the start." He lowered his voice. "Leanna was only 3 when her mother died, and she has a special closeness to my sister-in-law, Elizabeth. By myself I would have stayed and helped claim Texas, but the girls wouldn't have had enough folks around them."

We walked in silence for a while, then I stopped. "In her last letter, my sister, Betsey, asked me if my wandering feet will rest this side of the grave. I might ask you that question, Mr. Donner."

"My movings are over," he said. He looked deep into my eyes. "I find no place so much to my mind as this."

I held the gaze.

George Building His Wall, 1839

*O*ur courtship was brief, and more was not needed. It still sometimes surprises me that I, who had never planned to marry, married twice, and to two Southerners, both from North Carolina, both steady and measured, with honey voices and quick laughs. I have no doubt that my two husbands would have liked each other—sometimes I think George is exactly the kind of man Tully would have grown into had he lived.

I never expected nor tried to find another man after Tully, who valued me as much as himself, but the afternoon I watched George build the stone wall where his farm faced the road, I knew I would marry him. He spread a tarp on the ground, a quilt over that, near an apple tree, and we ate fresh apples and talked easily.

"I'm very fond of stone fences, Mr. Donner," I said. "They're unusual in this part of the country."

"My father is fond of them too," he said. "When I was a boy, he talked often about them. He was a militiaman in New Hampshire, and they saved his life more than once." He laughed. "Anyone can build a stone fence in the East. It's much more of a challenge here."

A large pile of stones of all sizes lay next to a cart filled with more stones, some he had wrested from a fallow field, others left over from the new statehouse in Springfield. He went regularly to Springfield to hear the Members of the Legislature speak, and asked if I'd like to accompany him sometime. After mentioning with amusement that one well-known Member was a charlatan and a windbag, he wasn't sure which was worse, he became engrossed in the work. I must admit I quickly stopped correcting my papers and became engrossed in watching him.

He looked carefully at the partially finished wall, looked at the stones that ranged from perhaps five pounds to fifty, then back at the wall, before selecting a stone from the pile. He lifted the huge boulders easily—and I have always admired physical strength manifested with grace in a man—yet he chose the smaller stones with a craftsman's care, testing the heft of the stone in his hands, feeling its planes and grooves, before choosing the place on the wall he wanted it to be, several times trying one, two, or three places before being satisfied. He checked both sides of the wall for precision. "Each stone should cast a shadow," he said. He didn't build the wall in order—in some places it was a foot high, two feet in others—the stones determined its order. "It's really an art, Mr. Donner," I said. "It's pretty simple, Mrs. Dozier," he said. "One over two, two over one." He was in no hurry nor rush—I would come to understand that he cared more about the building than the completion—and my heart said, I will cast my lot with this calm, deliberative man who cares about the fit and rightness of things.

A month later when he asked, "Mrs. Dozier, could you ever see your way into a future with me?" I answered readily, "I am already there, Mr. Donner."

Jan 22nd 1847

*I*n the beginning of course we were on ground level, but now we are underground inside walls of snow. We're not sure how much snow has fallen—twenty feet?—but from the poles Jean Baptiste thrusts into the ground, we estimate the snowpack at twelve feet. Near the opening of our shelter, we began with three carved snow stairs, and now there are eleven. George figured out an ingenious plan. After a storm, I pace out the number of steps from "the fireplace" to our "front door," then Jean Baptiste, whose stride is not much longer than mine, scrambles up through "the fireplace," paces out the same number of steps across the roof, shovels till he reaches our snow stairs, and then we make more stairs as needed. It sounds easy, but it often takes much of the day because George can no longer shovel and we all move slower now.

Now that Shoemaker, Smith, and Reinhardt are dead, Jean Baptiste is the only one left in the teamsters' shelter. Many nights he sleeps on a hide in front of our fire. I think he is more lonely than afraid. Sometimes when I glance up, he is looking at me and quickly casts his eyes down. His eyes are sad, and you can read every feeling he has on his face. I would prefer to be alone, but he does not bother me. Still, it is a relief when he goes to the lake camp for a day or two.

Jan 26th 1847

*J*ean Baptiste brought the sad news that Lewis Keseberg, Jr., is dead, the baby I delivered at Alcove Springs, Kansas, the day Margret Reed's mother, Sarah Keyes, died. I pulled back the wagon cover and said, "You have a son, Mr. Keseberg. The first American born on the Trail! What a lucky boy he is!"

In the ever-growing list of **Deaths**, I recorded today the pitiful short span of **Lewis Keseberg, Jr., d. Jan 24th 1847** at the lake camp. The baby who leavened our grief over Sarah Keyes's death and was a symbol of our future.

Before I knew it, Betsey, that dashed hope of the future spun me to dashed hopes of the past.

1831

Our son Thomas was born Oct 1st 1830, and a more beautiful little boy you never saw. Perfect strangers comment on how bonny he is, and the more people coo at him, the more frequent his smiles, until any passerby who bends down will be greeted with a smile that even the hardest heart could not resist. With his red hair and brown eyes, he doesn't favor anyone on our side at all, but is a template of his father.

"If he lives," I told Tully, "I very much desire that he have a Northern education."

Thomas Eustis Dozier d Sept 28th 1831 at home in Elizabeth City, North Carolina. Beloved son of Tully and Tamsen Eustis Dozier.

.   .   .

My head down on the Bible, I felt a little tugging on my skirt, and Eliza said, "Why are you crying, Momma?"

"I was thinking of Baby Lewis Keseberg and my little Thomas and all the children," I said.

She crawled up into my lap. "Poor little children," she said.

"Eliza, you are my comfort child in my troubles," I said. All my children are comforts to me, but Eliza, only 3, besides being so attuned to Georgia's moods, is almost preternaturally sensitive to others' feelings. It is a gift that will be both blessing and sorrow for her.

My children are alive. I have five *living* children to care for. What is wrong with me? I have never felt so vulnerable. What luck? What luck? I hear some part of myself calling, and the unbidden answer comes, No luck, no luck. The sorrows of the past mark us and stay in our hearts, but I must pull myself together to prevent sorrows of the future.

Personal History for the Children

When I was 6, my mother died. Betsey has told me that I became withdrawn, that even Father couldn't console me. I remember nothing of that, regrettably nothing of my mother either, except that her hands were small like mine. I can look at my hands now and see my mother's hands turning the pages of the books she read me.

A little over a year later, Father married Hannah Cogswell.

Shortly after that country road walk with George, I invited Elitha and Leanna to a tea party. I used my best rose-patterned china cups, and served sweets and savories. They sat erect and reserved in their Sunday dresses.

"Do you have a picture of your mother?" I asked.

Elitha opened the gold locket she still wears about her neck. I examined the picture of Mary Blue, a young, pretty woman with lively eyes, who died in childbirth along with the infant.

"You both carry her face," I said, closing the locket. "You favor your aunt Elizabeth too."

"Aunt Elizabeth is our mother's sister," Leanna said, looking straight at me.

"Sometimes an aunt can be like a mother," I said.

We sipped tea for a while.

"My mother died when I was 6," I said. "My stepmother loved me as if I were her own child."

And I've loved Elitha and Leanna the same way.

I was educated in Newburyport, Massachusetts, mainly by

GABRIELLE BURTON

my brother William's tutors. My maternal grandfather, Jeremiah Wheelwright, had been a schoolmaster in the 1700s, and education was highly valued in our household. That grandfather, whom I never met, served in the Revolutionary War under General Benedict Arnold—not yet a traitor. He died at 46 of exposure to cold, something I try not to think closely about.

I have told my daughters, "You come from illustrious people, but they are on the Atlantic Coast and you are on the Pacific, so your future depends upon your own merit and exertions."

I was a quick learner and avid student. I would be rich now if I had a penny for every time a tutor or Father said, "If only you'd been a boy, you'd go to Harvard, you'd be this, you'd be that . . ." They meant well, but the remark always riled me inside. The mind is like angels, neither male nor female, and I've never understood why people find that simple fact so difficult to grasp.

George is not bookish and makes no pretense to be, but he is my superior in temperament. I have struggled my whole life to tame my quick temper and curb my impatience. I have told our daughters to look for a steady temperament in their future mates. A man subject to sudden shifts in mood may be romantic in a novel, but makes a difficult husband who will require more care than their children.

I started teaching when I was 15. I taught mathematics, geometry, and general subjects.

"I heard you once taught surveying to a group of surprised young gentlemen, Mrs. Dozier," George said on that Springfield country road.

"It's been my general experience that gentlemen surprise far too easily, Mr. Donner."

"Not this gentleman," George said, and though I merely replied, "Good," my heart was smiling.

When I was 18, I traveled to Maine for a teaching job. There were nine families there, and I had twenty scholars. I enjoyed myself highly and might be there still had not the regular school-teacher unexpectedly recovered from his illness. Back in Massachusetts, still deep in recession, I cast about for teaching jobs and was compelled again to leave home and Betsey and Father, though not at such a great distance as before.

Then in 1824, when I had just turned 23, with Father's and Betsey's blessing I answered an advertisement for a teaching job in North Carolina, sailing there on a great ship at a time when many people thought that respectable women didn't travel alone. For the benefit of those who may wish to follow my example and encounter similarly ignorant people today, I leave it on record that, far from considering me an outlaw, people of all stamps on that ship from the Senator, Author, & Southern planter treated me with attention & respect. In my lifetime people have sometimes wondered at my conduct, but they have never despised me. And I never shall be despised. Most people, properly so, are quite indifferent to me. As Betsey once sagely told me: Others think much less about us than we believe or fear, because they are almost always thinking about themselves.

It was in North Carolina that I buried my first husband, my son, and a daughter almost at full term in 1831, and struggled on alone, able to survive only because I had a profession. My brother, William, was living in Illinois, and after his wife died in 1836, he asked me to emigrate there to take care of and educate his children. I went—leaving a school worth five hundred dollars a year—because I knew how he suffered, although William acted as if he were doing me a favor. My surroundings were of little concern to me. Much to my surprise, I met and married George Donner. How glad I am that I went to Springfield. Had I stayed where I was, repeating the same familiar life day after day, a narrow house would have been my home.

And so my road, which began in Massachusetts, went to Maine, back to Massachusetts, to North Carolina, to Illinois, to meet with George Donner's road at that juncture, the two of us then wending our way together on the California Trail almost two thousand miles west, is now temporarily stopped by ill circumstances. We have spent nearly three months trapped in the mountains with rescue yet to come.

Later

It occurs to me that when I write down George's and my history for the children, I may be revealing a belief or a fear that I may not be there to tell it to them.

John Landrum Murphy, 16, d. Jan 31st 1847 at the lake camp

This morning I bundled up Frances, Eliza, and Georgia, anxious to get them outside, really to go outside myself, away from the gloom and the smell of sickness. "Come, children, we'll walk Uno and visit Aunt Elizabeth." Elitha was sleeping, and when I asked Leanna if she wanted to go, she said, "No, thank you, Mother." I know from my own hardheaded mistakes that she suffers as much as Elizabeth or more. I heard my stepmother say, "Pity the instruction experience gives us can so rarely be transferred," and I let Leanna be.

Uno, all bone and rib cage, frisked in the snow and started digging. Halfway across the drifts to Elizabeth's shelter, Georgia stopped to stare at a foot sticking out of the snow. Samuel Shoemaker, one of our drivers, 25 years old, the first young man to go. I took Georgia's hand, guided her on.

As always the snow soaked our skirts, weighing them down—if we raise them, our stockings get soaked—and we had to struggle some, the children stepping into my footprints, but the brisk, sunny day and the exercise perked them up. Eliza hummed a little singsong, "We'll see Uncle Jacob and Aunt Elizabeth and all our cousins."

I stopped just outside the hole leading into the ground. "Uncle Jacob doesn't live here anymore, Eliza, but we'll see the rest."

On the flight of snow stairs leading down into the ground, Eliza grimaced. "Bad smell," she said. She wouldn't budge. "Come out here, cousins," she called. "Out here."

A feral-faced child, my niece Mary, 7, came from behind the

hanging canvas, squinting in the light. She reached out a dirty hand to Eliza. Eliza recoiled, darted behind me, and began crying.

Mary started crying and disappeared behind the canvas, where someone else was crying.

I looked at Frances, who without a word took her little sisters' hands.

"I'll take you home and we'll have a lovely tea party," Frances said.

I watched the children and Uno trudge back across the clearing.

Disappear underground.

I don't want to go in either, Eliza, I thought, walked down the snow stairs, and pushed aside the canvas, calling, "Elizabeth," but of course no one answered.

She was crying, and her children lay without moving on their platforms, while I stirred up the fire, untied a blue calico handkerchief, and poured bits of bone into a watery broth.

"These'll thicken the soup," I said. No flicker of interest from anyone. It crossed my mind that I might have saved them for my own family.

I gave my niece and nephews small pieces of bark and twigs of pine. "Chew on these. They'll make you less hungry."

My nephew William kept his back to me. "William, go out and help Jean Baptiste retrieve the wood."

Each storm Jean Baptiste must climb higher up the trees to cut limbs that hurl down into the snow and have to be dug out and dragged and chopped.

"William."

He reluctantly got up and started toward the stairs.

"Where's Solomon?" I asked.

"Gone," Elizabeth said.

"Gone? Gone where?"

"He set out for the settlements this morning," William said angrily. "I wanted to go, but Mother wouldn't let me."

"Solomon said, 'I'm not going to die like Landrum Murphy,'" Elizabeth said. "Now he'll just die alone."

"Elizabeth, kneel with me."

I took Elizabeth's hand, tugged her up, and the two of us knelt together. "The Lord is my shepherd," I said. "He maketh me to lie down in green pastures. He leadeth me— Say it, Elizabeth. He leadeth me"—I waited until she finally joined me—"out by cool waters and reviveth my drooping spirit. Though I walk through the valley of death, I fear not, for I dwell in the house of the Lord. He dost spread a banquet for me—"

Walking slowly back home, I piled snow on the partially exposed foot and packed it down. I took one of the poles Jean Baptiste probes the snow with searching for buried oxen, tied the blue calico kerchief on it like a small, bright flag, and thrust it into the snow to mark the spot where Samuel lies. "Rest in peace, Samuel."

On a log outside our shelter, Frances handed two rose-patterned china cups full of snow to Georgia and Eliza. Her china cup had a mended handle.

"I've fixed us all a lovely cup of custard," she said. With a silver spoon, Frances took a dainty bite of snow and smacked her lips in relish. "Delicious."

Georgia and Eliza followed suit.

As I passed the girls, Frances looked up and said quickly, "We're being careful with your china, Momma."

"You're good girls," I said and went into the shelter.

My precious china.

My Little Frances

*F*rances Eustis Donner, b. July 8th 1840

As the middle child, Frances has had her pick of age, going up with her big sisters or down to be one of "the babies"—the latter choice not often exercised anymore. She has always been mature for her age. I have to be careful not to ask too much of her.

Physically, they say she favors me most of my three youngest daughters. I feel that is another indication that people do not observe with care, but even George says it is true. If so, then it is I who is complimented. Even when I was Frances's age, my hair was never as golden or curly as hers.

Now all our hair is limp and lackluster. I started braiding mine on the Trail so as not to have to fuss with it, though George used to love watching me brush it at night, and sometimes brushed it for me. Either Elitha or I braid all the children's hair daily.

While her four sisters have black hair and dark brown eyes and skin that browns like wheat grain in the summertime, Frances and I have blue eyes and fair skin and always have to try to remember our sunbonnets. But Frances's eyes are a true cornflower blue, while mine are lighter blue. I was told so often when I was younger that my sharp gaze made people uncomfortable that, with time and practice, I learned to moderate it, simply pull a shade back and look at people from behind that. It is with dismay that I have watched Frances's pure, guileless gaze become penetrating, knowing. She is 6 and a half and has old eyes.

She's a curious, observant child, but also one who keeps part of herself private. I would not be surprised at all if she became an artist.

On the Trail one day George took a reed, cut off its shoots with his penknife, burnt holes at regular intervals with a coal, and made a whistle. Much to all our delight, but especially Frances's, he played "Buffalo Gals." The whistle had a happy, round sound, and often we'd hear Frances inside the wagon playing little cheerful tunes that made anyone within earshot smile.

When she lies on her rack and plays the whistle here, it only sounds mournful, conjuring up lonesome prairies, vast empty spaces. Yesterday she played "Buffalo Gals" over and over like a dirge, and when Leanna asked her to please stop, I was glad.

Sometimes Georgia and Eliza weep, Eliza fastening her arms tightly around Frances's neck, hiding her eyes against her shoulder. "Shhh," Frances says, until they're calmed.

She never cries, never complains. She often whispers to her doll, and I pray Dolly is her confidante.

February

1847

Feb 3rd 1847

$\mathcal{J}$ean Baptiste, looking for game shortly after dawn, found my nephew Solomon Hook in the woods close to camp, snow-blind with his mind unbalanced. He had been gone forty-eight hours, circling around all that time.

Later

This morning, after applying cold compresses to Solomon's eyes to relieve the sting, I made eye patches from padded muslin. We had to tie his hands to keep him from rubbing his poor swollen, bloodshot eyes. He says he saw halos around everything and his eyes feel full of sand. I remember that one of Father's men suffering similarly from looking directly at the solar eclipse made a complete recovery, and I pray this will be so with Solomon.

This afternoon, Solomon calm and resting, I was walking back from Elizabeth's shelter, so relieved to be done there for the day. The sun, sparkling on the snow, had thawed the top layer, my feet going *crunch crunch* as they broke through the crust. Do you remember how I used to break the thin layer of ice on puddles and Mother scolded me for ruining my shoes and scolded you for letting me? I saw Elitha and Leanna come out from our shelter to gather the bedding they had put out to air earlier, the sound of their feet breaking the snow *crunch crunch* sailing across the clearing, and just like that I was in the Great Salt Lake Desert.

.   .   .

Crunch, *Elitha, Leanna, and I stagger alongside a wagon, its wheels bog down in the salty crust, our shoes break through the crust* crunch, *the sun sparkles off the salt crystals so brightly it hurts our inflamed eyes, the gritty dust pelts us, I blink my eyes. Blink again.*

Twenty women with forty girls walk in the same direction we do. I put my hand on Elitha and Leanna and stop.

The twenty women do the same.

I raise my hand in salute.

The twenty women salute.

Father told me that sometimes after weeks at sea, only water building and rolling, building and rolling, he saw mirages, once an island nearby that never materialized, staying in front of them for days, never getting closer, until it suddenly vanished as quickly as it had appeared. A trick of the mind, Father said, manifesting your desires, your hopes.

Standing stock-still in the clearing this afternoon, recalling the mirage or vision I saw in the desert, watching my daughters coping so heroically, I was filled with a fierce hope. We *will* get them out of here, and California *will* be advantageous for them. In a new land, they can act for themselves. They can *act*. For an instant I felt at one with all the women through time who walked their own unbroken trails, preparing the way for me and my daughters and their daughters and their . . .

I raised my hand in a part wave, part salute to Elitha and Leanna. It seemed an oddly solemn gesture as I did it, and I can't tell you if it was triumphant or defiant or both. They waved or saluted back, and began gathering bedding off the ground.

Feb 4th dawn

Sometimes I wonder if I am going mad. My feelings change constantly, my thoughts collide. I see things. Shapes. Several times at night, I lifted my head up from my writing and saw the shadows move, although everyone was motionless on their platforms. Are we so close to death a veil is lifting? Is death coming to take us? Or is this what hunger does?

I was born with a caul on my face, so some of the old people said I had second sight. I've never felt I had any special gift, I just think I pay more attention than many. But my senses have grown very keen here. Every day they seem to refine more.

Last night after I saw the shadows, I lay on my platform and listened to the children breathe, pacing my own breath to theirs, as if I could will their bodies to hold on steadily.

As if I could breathe for them while they sleep, guarding their lives from the moving shadows.

As if I could breathe life into them.

Night

 $\mathcal{E}$ ven here at the table I can hear Elitha's teeth grinding. I don't have to walk over there to see her lick her lips, open her mouth, groan, lick her lips, open her mouth . . . She dreams about food, the recurrent dream we all have of tantalizing food we can see, smell, that comes to our very lips, but always always always something interferes that prevents the food from reaching our mouths.

Jean Baptiste is staying at Elizabeth's for a while. He is the only one strong enough to restrain Solomon when he goes into one of his rages.

5th

*U*no ate one of Frances's shoes. In a sudden temper that startled him as well as us, George cuffed Uno, immediately regretting it, and tried to soothe the cowering dog while I calmed the crying children. I gave Frances one of my shoes, and we stuffed the toes with paper. I will wear one of Elizabeth's, because she no longer goes out.

Later we also cut paper to pad the holes in the other children's shoes with old copies of the *Sangamo Journal* that we had used for packing. I was remembering a faraway time and place when I wrapped china in these same papers and Allen Francis balled them up to fill the spaces in our crates.

"My sister, Betsey, writes that Thoreau has retreated to Walden Pond," I said, *"but goes a mile down the road every night to his mother's for dinner."*

Allen laughed. "Everyone doesn't have to go twenty-five hundred miles to find what he wants."

"It's true I have a taste for travel," I said, and then we laughed again. George looked up from wrapping a plate, looked back down.

"To carve out a new home, a new country!" Allen said. "How lucky you are! What a book you will write! Now remember. Send me every detail. My readers will be eager for them, but none so much as I."

I handed George another shoe and some newspapers and said, "Do you remember Allen Francis saying when we had nothing to do we could read these papers in California? I look at them now, and they might as well be in a foreign language."

George laid the paper on the platform, weighted it with the shoe, cut strips with his left hand for a while, and then said quietly, almost abashed, "I was a little jealous of Allen Francis."

"Whatever for?"

George kept his eyes on the paper. "You shared a world with him. All those books I've never read. Writing poetry—"

I looked at him, amazed. "I share many worlds with you. The children are whole universes you and I share. Our love of travel and adventure . . ." I smiled ruefully. "This place."

He looked up. "This is none of my business . . . You don't have to answer if you don't—"

"What?" I said.

"Is it true he asked you to marry him before I did?"

"Yes."

George looked at me then with such sadness I couldn't imagine what he was thinking.

I waited.

"If you had married him, you'd still be in Springfield," he said.

"Yes, I would," I said. "Allen was a rocking chair traveler." Suddenly a little laugh came out of me. "They'll never say that about us," I said.

And in the midst of dismal, dire surroundings, George and I laughed together.

Hope flares again.

Later

George wasted his worry. Yes, my friend Allen Francis and I were intellectually compatible. Allen was always stimulating— ideas, enthusiasms, and deadlines tumbling one after another—

that's what drew me to him. But while it thrilled me deeply that, in the East, Elizabeth Peabody published Margaret Fuller and Nathaniel Hawthorne, and although my own ideas often poured fervently from me, I think above all intellectual, philosophical, and spiritual inclination, I am as my father and uncle were before me: a sailor. I *will* be a sailor, I shouted to my father when I was just a bit of a girl, and I feel it has been the driving force of my life, the very essence of my soul.

And in George, I recognized a kindred soul, as well as a harbor.

Feb. 6th '47 more thaw

As our departure date drew closer, George and I were giddy with anticipation! It really was going to happen! We were going to California!

On one side of the general store, George and Jacob picked out tools and farm implements, George waving his hand at the knives, whetstones, axes, shovels, crowbars, awls, chain, nails, and practically crowing to Mr. Parsons, the storekeeper, "Tar to grease our wheels, and these to grease our land negotiations with the Mexicans!" "Aren't you worried they might kill you and your family, Mr. Donner?" Mr. Parsons said, shaking his head when George said, "Worried? This is Manifest Destiny!" "Some folks say it's just plain plunder," Parsons mumbled. "Yeah, I've heard that," George said, more amused than challenged. He gestured toward the huge pile of tools and implements. "We're paying for the land, Parsons," he said. "Why, you can't stop movement any more than you can stop ripe fruit falling from the tree. And who would want to? You might just as well say Christopher Columbus should have stayed home. Now we're going to need at least a dozen more shovels . . ." While across the store, just as exhilarated, Elizabeth and I chose bolts of silks, satins, laces, velvets for the Mexican ladies, and muslin, bright cotton prints, red and yellow flannels for the Indians.

Mrs. Parsons leaned across the counter and lowered her voice. "Can't you talk your husband out of this, Mrs. Donner?"

It took me a moment to get my wits back. "Mrs. Parsons. I want to go to California. Mr. Donner and I are certain it will be advantageous for us and for our children."

Mrs. Parsons harrumphed and turned to Elizabeth. "Aren't you afraid to take your children into the wilderness?" Elizabeth was taken aback too, *so I finally answered, "Fear didn't build this country, Mrs. Parsons. Remember, just a few years ago Illinois was wilderness."*

Now when we recall that day, George sees that Jacob hung back, leaving all the decisions to him, that Mr. Parsons shook his head, not in fear, as George had thought, but much more in censure, as if our whole enterprise was misguided or folly, and I see beyond Mrs. Parsons's clamped lips that Elizabeth was fidgety, almost querulous. She gestured to a bolt of red velvet. "Isn't that a little dear for the Mexican ladies?" I ran my fingers down it. "They won't be able to resist it."

Today Leanna picked up the bolt of red velvet and started to rip it. "Don't use that until we use everything else up," I said.

Working almost silently, the melting snow freezing our hands, George working with only one arm, we balled up linsey, muslin, and some iridescent green silk to stuff the holes in the ceiling. Where we've taken the hides off, the melting snow drips in. We are eating the roof over our heads.

When pain shot again across George's face from the effort, I pulled back Mrs. Wolfinger's curtain, put balled up silk in her hands, and pointed to the ceiling.

Afternoon

I looked up and saw Frances peeking at Mrs. Wolfinger through a gap in the blankets.

"Frances, come away from there," I said. "Give her privacy. That's her place, this is ours."

Frances came over to the table. "Why does she cry all the time?"

I heard the omnipresent mewling come from behind Mrs. Wolfinger's blanket then, only because Frances had called attention to it. Most of the time I don't even hear it.

"She's a long way from home," I said. "We all have each other. She has no one." I wrapped a strip of linen around a smooth stick, dipped it into a pan of warm water, and laved George's wound.

"And she doesn't understand our language," George said.

"Don't you speak her language?" Frances asked.

"I studied standard German with my brother's tutor for only a term," I said, "and to his regret, your father's parents wanted their children to speak only English. Mrs. Wolfinger speaks a dialect we barely understand."

"Why don't you teach her English?" Frances said.

"I tried, but she doesn't seem interested in learning."

Frances watched us for a while, gradually making her way back to Mrs. Wolfinger's blanket. I pretended not to notice how, very slyly, she slipped inside.

I have no idea what transpired, but for a blessed moment the crying stopped.

The Germans

*T*he Wolfingers, Joseph Reinhardt, and Augustus Spitzer joined our company in Independence. This is what we know about them.

Mr. Wolfinger, (first name?), 22–26?, had a well-equipped wagon and sturdy oxen. His new bride, Doris, had gold earbobs and a trunkful of brightly colored silk dresses that she changed often, once twice in one day, giving the gossips frequent occasion to wag their tongues. She was 19 but seemed much younger, a girl really, a very pretty girl who may not have had pretty things before. I enjoyed her simple pleasure and thought it a good thing she had a trunkful of those silk dresses, because silk soaked up stains and had to be sweltering. I brought worsted dresses, which didn't show soil or wrinkles, but oh, how they also retained the heat. The children's linsey dresses were much cooler—indeed, on the hot prairie, I often wished I had linsey. Odd for me now to recall being too hot, and odd too to write about Doris Wolfinger's trunkful of dresses, rotting now in one of the deserts, when for so many months she has worn the same tattered, stained, soiled red silk dress, even sleeping in it.

The Wolfingers camped adjacent to Lewis and Philippine Keseberg's two wagons, and next to them was the wagon shared by Joseph Reinhardt and Augustus Spitzer, both around 30, partners in a never specified business. Most people referred to them all as "the Germans," although Philippine Keseberg told me that her husband, Lewis, said the other Germans were common and forbade her to associate with them.

Once I walked by their wagons on my way out to the prairie to botanize, and Mr. Wolfinger had a proprietary hand on Mrs. Wolfinger's shoulder, while she held up her new wedding band to catch the sun's glints. It made me smile, but nearby, Mr. Reinhardt and Mr. Spitzer looked at the Wolfingers with sour envy. Mr. Spitzer swigged a flask of whiskey and handed it to Mr. Reinhardt, who spied me and tried to cover up the whiskey bottle. "Good day, Mrs. Donner," Mr. Reinhardt said in a fawning tone. Remember, I wrote you then, Betsey, "We have some of the best people in our company, and some too that are not so good." Really, I despise sneaks and toadies, but I disliked more Mr. Spitzer's bold stare, challenging me to chastise him, as if his vices were of concern to me.

June 16, 1846

Mr. Stanton and I have found the wild tulip, the primrose, the lupine, the eardrop, the larkspur, and creeping hollyhock, and a beautiful flower resembling the blossom of the beech tree, but in bunches as large as a small sugar loaf, and of every variety of shade, to red and green . . .

Phlox Carnea

"I told him it'd be just like the old days," George said.

He has said this more than once before, and I didn't answer. On my lap was a journal page I had ripped out and ruled into small squares, drawing a different trail flower on each: another card game to distract the children. I cut out the squares and watched George stare deeply into the fire.

"The old days," he said again and looked over at me. "He didn't want to go to Kentucky. He couldn't wait to get home from Texas. I dragged him to Illinois. He never wanted to try anything new.

"He and his first wife lived with us for a year before she insisted on getting their own farm.

"I used to plow his fields after I did mine."

I knew about the first wife and the fields, but the rest was news to me. I nodded, and the words burst out of George in a torrent, as if saved up for fifty years.

"My little brother. Ever since I can remember, he was bigger and stronger than I was, and he used to pommel me every other week, and I *still* felt responsible for him.

"Once I heard my mother say to her sister, 'Jacob and George are night and day.' I puzzled for years as to exactly what she meant.

"Before she died, Mother said, 'George, you watch out for your little brother.' It just seemed a natural request to me, and I promised, but now I think about it: Jacob was fifty-three years old!"

He talked for a long time, this happened in Texas, that happened in Kentucky, I should never . . . , and I just listened. From the first day I met him, Jacob was incurious and peevish, but I've kept my opinion to myself. Sometimes I had to force myself to be pleasant, and I did. You poke at blood ties at your own peril. As you well know, Betsey, I've lost my temper more than once with William, but woe betide anyone else who ever says a word against our brother.

To my amazement and George's deep pleasure, Jacob grew in strength and vigor in the first few months on the Trail. He and George rode ahead to scout camping sites; they hunted buffalo, racing at full tilt to present the bloody humps to Elizabeth and me. But he flagged noticeably in the Wasatch, and after the axle broke and the chisel slipped and gouged George's hand, he just gave up. One day at the table in their shelter, he laid his head down on his arms and wouldn't get up. Elizabeth was frantic. George tried to rouse him without success. "Jacob, listen to me. Milt Elliott is here. He and the others are going to walk over and bring things back. I've made a list of things we need. Jacob. Jacob."

Only once did Jacob respond. He lifted his head and said, "I'm sorry, George."

"My hand is nearly good as new," George said.

"I let you down again," Jacob said.

"You've never let me down, Jacob," George said, but Jacob never spoke to anyone again. He just laid his head on that table, leaving Elizabeth, and seven children, to drag the oxen hides in, search for wood, keep the fire going . . . I couldn't help thinking that a second husband had abandoned her.

But I will never forget that Jacob was the one who pulled my baby Eliza from the overturned wagon. When he lay motionless on his platform that last day, I whispered in his ear, "Thank you for saving Eliza. I will always be grateful."

I hope somewhere in his being he heard me.

My dearest sister,

I don't know what it's been like for others, but this is how it has been for me. It didn't really penetrate for some time that we were stopped here. In the beginning, I was concentrating on George's wound, what a wound like that means in our debilitated condition, planning how we'd keep it clean in the difficult trail conditions. That first snowstorm lasted eight days, and although George and I agreed that the shelter was sturdy enough, that firewood was plentiful, and that we could butcher all the oxen we could find, it still seemed a temporary delay like all the other ones along the Trail, and we were just waiting for it to be over so we could go on. One day, I whispered, "Oh my God," and it was part prayer, part sinking realization: We are trapped in the mountains.

Perhaps I knew it all along and it was just a matter of accepting it.

We're not the first. In '44, as Patrick Breen so often reminded the men at the campfires, a young man from the Stevens Party had to spend the winter in the mountains. We knew his name, Moses Schallenberger, as well as an old acquaintance. Does it strike anyone else as morbidly amusing that the Breens claimed the cabin that Moses built? That young man from the Stevens Party of '44 was a cautionary tale for all the emigrants of '45 and '46—as we have become another cautionary tale to be told at campfires from now on, hurry hurry—but for us here in the mountains he has become a tale of hope, because we know it's possible to survive.

It's only in the middle of the night that doubt comes.

But that's not true either. My feelings change a dozen times in the same day. I keep us all on a strict schedule to keep a tight rein on them.

What is hardest for me, Betsey, is having no one to tell my fears to, so they can be shared or assuaged. George and I talk all the time, but I cannot burden him with my fears. They would pull him down, and he is already struggling. If I didn't have you to tell everything to, I couldn't bear it.

I struggle too. Sometimes I feel almost a hatred for Mrs. Wolfinger. She is alone in a foreign land, the man who brought her here murdered by her compatriots. But she has built a country of one inside. I tried to teach her English, but she stayed mute, willfully mute it seemed to me after a while. I don't have the energy to take care of everyone. Because I insist she contribute, she gathers firewood sullenly, immediately retreating behind her curtain. She makes no attempt to keep clean. She comes out only for her bowl of hides, and I have begun to resent every bite she takes. I know some of what she feels. After Tully died, I wanted to lie down and die. But you have to pull yourself together. Or lie down and die and stop taking food out of my children's mouths.

God forgive me, I am becoming cruel. I do not want to be the kind of person I'm becoming.

"None of us knows what we'll do until we're tested," George said.

Feb 7th 1847

This morning was the second time Elitha refused to wash and I said she must.

"What does it matter?" she said. "We're like beasts in a cave."

Betsey, this is a child with such a strong sense of aesthetics she retied ribbons on her baby sisters' birthday presents. Even if we were canning jam or slopping the hogs, she insisted on wearing a fresh pinafore daily.

"Look at your father," I said sharply. At the table, George, one arm useless, laboriously shaved with the other while Frances held up the mirror Grandmother gave me. "We're not beasts in a cave, Elitha. Even if we have to force ourselves, we have to remember who we are and act that way. We have to act as if this is temporary, because it is."

I gave her the speech I give myself frequently, and I said it loudly enough for Mrs. Wolfinger to hear.

Reluctantly Elitha got up and washed her face and hands, to my relief.

She is taller than I am. I could not have physically forced her to wash. I suppose it is a kind of blessing that hunger makes resistance harder. It is just too much effort. I'm glad of that but also regretful; it's not in my children's natures to mindlessly follow orders.

I marvel at George. He shaves *every single day*. My biggest battle is inertia. As it is, it's hard for me to concentrate. Sometimes my hand shakes. I hope this is legible.

Night

"Tell me again what Illinois is like, Momma," Frances asked this afternoon.

If I had looked at George, I think I would have burst into tears. I took a deep breath and kept my voice normal. "In spring, our farm in Illinois looked like a garden, remember? Fifty peach trees in bloom along with the cherry and the pear. Behind the farmhouse—remember?—we had a whole orchard of fruit trees with their clusters of flowers. The peach trees bloomed first, and when the wind blew their blossoms, you stood under the trees with your big sisters and caught handfuls. Aunt Elizabeth and I spent days canning peaches and pears for wintertime, and you helped. Then came my favorite, the apple trees in full flower. The apple blossoms were at their height the day in May your father and I married, the bees humming in the pink and white blossoms . . ."

Jean Baptiste, sitting at my feet, was enthralled, as were the children. For a moment, the dank shelter seemed to be filled with white apple blossoms sailing through the air, sailing—

"Why did we leave?" Frances asked.

The blossoms became snow dripping through the top where we're taking the hides down. George and I looked at each other, then turned away.

$\mathcal{W}$e left, dear Frances, because I wanted to leave.

My reading group began Hastings's book the very night James Reed brought it, and my eagerness to go overland, already keen, grew. After my group left, George and I talked at the kitchen table.

"It's one thing to read about it," George said. "I relish reading about it. But we can't just pick up and go."

"Why not?"

George laughed. "For one thing, I'm too old—"

I raised an eyebrow. "Not you."

"Well, the children are too young—"

"Now which one is it, George? You're too old or they're too young? It's not like it's '44 or '45. There's a trail to California, plain to be seen. Wagons have done it. We know what to expect."

We continued the conversation around the clock, Betsey. There were genuine concerns about such a venture, and I had already thought long and hard about them.

Milking cows in the barn, George said, "We would leave a great deal behind. All my grown children and grandchildren—"

"They can come with us if they want. I would delight in their company, but they all seem content where they are."

"You're not?"

"You know I love it here, but it's so . . . *settled*. California's the last frontier, George. Don't you want to see it, be part of it?"

When George couldn't keep the hankering off his face, we both burst out laughing.

In the bedroom, dark except for one candle, in our night-clothes, he said, "Tamsen, I could never leave Jacob."

"Of course not," I said. "They'll come with us. Jacob can live out his years in warmth and sunshine, and Elizabeth can find a thousand new things to cook. Imagine the opportunities for all our children, George, what their lives will be like. What *our* lives will be like!"

"All that free land," George mused again the next night in the bedroom, and looked at me and grinned. "All you want just there for the taking—"

"I'll start my school for girls!"

"In a few years, California will be like Illinois," George said. "We'll be in on it from the beginning!"

We embraced, George snuffed out the candle, and we fell back on the bed.

The next four months were a pleasure of preparation and anticipation, Betsey. In March, one month before departure, we had stopped at Elizabeth and Jacob's to show them all the new parcels. One parcel had beautiful new boots for George, and of course he wanted to show Jacob right away.

In the barn, three wagons were in various stages of construction. Jacob's stepsons, Solomon and William, and two teamsters, Samuel Shoemaker and James Smith, packed shiny farm implements. Jacob rested on a haystack, his eyes closed.

George strode into the barn with a pack of smaller nephews. "See my new boots, Jacob. Aren't they beauties?"

Jacob opened his eyes and gave a token nod.

George showed them to Solomon and William and to the teamsters, who whistled approval, then he picked up a sack of seed off a pile near Jacob. "You know, boys," he said to his nephews, "in California you just throw the seed on the ground and reach down and pick the plant. What do you fancy to eat, Jacob?"

Jacob slowly shook his head. "I think I'm just gonna stay put."

George's face sobered, but his tone was still light. "All you can look forward to here is snow freezing your privates."

Our nephews giggled. Jacob's fleeting smile looked like a grimace. "I'm too old, my legs hurt, my back," he whined. "My whole life I've had pain, George——"

In the doorway I held two blueberry pies Elizabeth had sent out and watched George listening to Jacob's litany, watched him deflate with every ailment. "Oh, for heaven's sake, Jacob," I finally said, "you'll live twenty more years in warmth and sunshine."

Jacob lumbered to get up, groaning in an exaggerated way.

I knew George would not go without him. "If you don't want to go for yourself, Jacob," I said, "go for your children. Don't rob them of this opportunity."

Chagrined, Jacob looked at his boys' pleading faces. He looked at George. "You really think I could do it?"

"All you need is a little open country," George said. He reached out a hand and pulled Jacob up. "It'll be just like the old days, brother."

George turned to me tonight and said, "I knew he didn't want to go. I talked him into it, because otherwise I couldn't have come."

"You didn't act alone," I said.

Feb 8th 1847

"What luck?" the rower shouted to the ship, and we waited, breaths held, until the answer came.

"We had bad luck," Jean Baptiste says frequently.

I've thought often about luck here. We always assign a value to luck, think it either good or bad. Looked at that way, he's right. Luck was against us.

But you also can retrace our steps, as I have done many nights, and see that many small decisions, made thoughtfully or without thought, carried us incrementally, inexorably, here. You could say, though I'm not ready to, that we caused our own fate.

June 1831, North Carolina

Tully stands at the window with Thomas on his shoulders and spreads his arms wide. "See your farm, Thomas," he says. At this time of day, the light is golden, and I know he looks at a delightful sight. "And your mother is eager to go to Ohio," Tully says incredulously. He turns around to where I'm writing you at the table. "Tell your sister that no one in her right mind would ever leave such abundance. Carolina has every delight anyone could want."

Carolina *was* a beautiful place, Betsey, and I was very happy there. Our farm and my school prospered, and I was quite the entrepreneur, selling our milk and eggs at the door, honey from our bees, and my special molded butter. I know you have many wonders in Newburyport, but I rather think you don't have butter designs. In the evenings, I took the butter from the cold water crocks in our storehouse and laid out my tools: a circular wooden board Tully had fashioned for me, a set of sharply pointed sticks, a knife, and squares of muslin. While Tully rocked Thomas to sleep and we talked quietly by candlelight, I molded designs on the butters: flowers, a bird, whatever took my fancy, once even an elephant, squeezing a lump of butter through the muslin for its rough skin, a different muslin mesh for its tail, and my knife blade for its tusks. I did not charge extra for the designs because molding gave me pleasure, but I couldn't make enough butter to keep up with the demand.

Yet, every time I bid one of our Ohio-bound neighbors farewell, desire leapt in me. All my life, I have wondered about the place I'm not in. You either are that way or you aren't, and you can't imagine the opposite state.

Tully wasn't that way—though we had determined to re-move to some western state the next year because of his precari-ous health and our strong dislike to slavery—and there were times I found it hard to want something and have to wait for someone else to want it too. George was, though he thought he had grown too old.

I will own the truth. I wanted George and the children to go to California because I couldn't go without them. But I wanted them to go for themselves too. It cannot be wrong to wish as much for others as you wish for yourself. Certainly it can't be wrong to wish things for yourself.

I would give anything to take upon myself the pain my chil-dren now endure. It is nearly intolerable to consider that I may be responsible for that pain.

Feb 9th 1847

$\mathcal{M}$y menses have stopped. I thought it was the change of life, but this morning Elitha told me hers have stopped too. In one way I'm glad, because it's easier, but it worries me too. What else is shutting down in our bodies?

The darkness has bothered me the most. It can be high noon outside, but here, underground, it's always dark. We read and write and eat and live by lighted pinecones when Jean Baptiste can find them in the snow and the omnipresent firelight, which casts its eerie shadows in the corners. I tell myself, Betsey, that this is just like when I was little and we ate by firelight and candlelight because the whale oil was too precious to use, but it's not like that at all because I didn't know anything different then. When the snow melts more, Jean Baptiste and I hope to uncover one of our wagons to find kerosene lamps, and my sewing box for Elitha to bring back her interest, which has flagged again now that the tobacco is gone.

Solomon came over today. With a hat shading his eyes, he was able to tolerate the bright light. He seems his old self, and his visit cheered up everyone. Jean Baptiste asked me if he could come back home, and I said yes.

Feb 10th '47

"*T*he third wagon has all the things we won't need until California," Frances says, parroting my voice.

Enormously excited, she, Georgia, and Eliza, in linsey traveling dresses, peep out the window at the three pristine covered wagons in our farmyard.

"The second has our food, our clothes, all the necessities of camp life."

They squeal and jump up and down, watching oxen, horses, dogs, their father, and the teamsters engage in tremendous activity. Next to the children, an 1846 feed store calendar left on the wall has a date circled in red: April 15.

"And the first wagon," Frances tells her sisters, "is our family home on wheels!"

We dismantled the first wagon and parts of the other two for the shelter, platforms, table, benches, and a small "cupboard" near the fireplace we kept the food in until it was gone.

The remnants of the second and third wagons are encased in snow that thaws and freezes, but this afternoon, Jean Baptiste tunneled like a madman and reached one.

"Tamsen," George yelled from his platform. "The seed!"

I turned around wearily.

"Don't you remember?" he said, already struggling to get up. "In California you just throw the seed on the ground, boys. What do you fancy to eat, Jacob?"

George in between us, Jean Baptiste and I stumbled across the clearing until George said, "Here. We're close, I know we're close."

Jean Baptiste thrust a pole into the ground. It struck something. He looked at George.

"Keep going! Keep going!"

Jean Baptiste shoveled, then clawed at the snow with his bare hands until he uncovered wood. He smiled hugely at us, almost crazily I thought, until I realized later that our smiles back mirrored his.

Jean Baptiste wriggled down the tunnel he'd made. George and I looked at each other, holding our breath.

Jean Baptiste emerged, exultant, holding a bag of seed.

Even with one arm, George easily tore open the soggy bag. His face immediately fell. He stared at the black, withered seed, shaking his head in disbelief and disappointment.

Inside the children gathered round me at the fireplace as I ferociously stirred the contents of the pot as if I could will it into something they could eat. George touched my shoulder.

"It's blighted, Tamsen. You can't salvage it."

I stared at the fetid, black, oozing liquid, which was clearly inedible.

"Can you fix it, Mother?" Frances asked.

Feb 11th

Today Leanna slapped Elitha, who slapped her back.

"Stop it!" I yelled. "Stop it this instant!" When we had all calmed down, I gathered the whole family and said, "Until rescue comes, our only hope of survival is each other. We have to help each other—"

"She never stops talking about food," Leanna said.

"I'm sorry," Elitha said, "I just can't help it."

"Yes, you can," I said. "You're stronger than you think."

"I'm sorry I slapped you," Leanna said. "Sometimes I feel wild, as if I'm going to burst into a thousand pieces."

Then both of them cried and hugged each other, and I thought, I know the precise feeling, Leanna.

Harriet McCutchen, 1, d. Feb 2nd 1847 at the lake camp. At Fort Bridger when George said the McCutchens were welcome to join us, "Big Bill" lifted Harriet, delicate as a Dresden doll, over his head with one hand. "We're goin' to California, Punkin!" She laughed with glee.

Margaret "Maggie" Eddy, 1, d. Feb 4th 1847 at the lake camp

Eleanor Eddy, 25, d. Feb 7th 1847 at the lake camp (Husband and father, William Eddy, went with the snowshoers Dec 16th '46. No word yet.)

Augustus Spitzer, 30?, d. Feb 8th 1847 at the lake camp. From Germany. Joseph Reinhardt's partner?

George shook his head. "With both Reinhardt and Spitzer dead," he said, "we'll never know what happened to Wolfinger in the second desert."

Oct. 6–13th 1846
Wolfinger Disappears

*B*efore we set out, Betsey, we knew we had to cross a forty-mile desert between the Humboldt River and the Truckee River to get to California. We also knew that Hastings Cutoff involved a "dry drive."

"Thirty miles," Hastings said the "dry drive" was.

It was eighty.

"Two days and two nights," he said.

It was six days and six nights.

We crossed the "dry drive," the Great Salt Lake Desert, September 4–9th 1846. The Reeds lost two wagons, the Kesebergs one, we lost one. Thirty-six head of working cattle vanished. James Reed lost his entire herd, except for one ox and one cow. Once the most prosperous, now he had least of all. He had to promise two for one in California to Mr. Breen and Mr. Graves for two scrawny oxen that could barely drag the big family wagon along.

In the second desert in October, the Indians shot more cattle. The Eddys abandoned their only wagon; they had no oxen to draw it. Mr. Eddy, carrying three-year-old Jimmy, and his wife, Eleanor, carrying baby Maggie, walked the forty miles. I left my crate of books, so painstakingly chosen for my new school, keeping only Dickens for Eliza. But we reached the Truckee River; from then on, we would never be out of reach of water. We had all gotten across, except for the Wolfingers' wagon, which was expected soon.

. . .

*Mrs. Wolfinger woke George at dawn, and a few moments later, he roused me.
"Wolfinger's young bride is very upset. I can't make out what she's saying."*

*She was hysterical, nearly unintelligible. I held her very firmly and
told her several times in German to speak slower, until I made out the gist
and turned to George. "She says her husband never came in."*

*Mr. Spitzer and Mr. Reinhardt weren't in yet either, but Mr. Keseberg
said everyone was getting upset over nothing. "They will be helping
Wolfinger cache his goods," Mr. Keseberg said. "They will catch up."*

*That made sense, because after Mr. Spitzer and Mr. Reinhardt abandoned their wagon in the first desert, they had thrown their few bundles
into Mr. Wolfinger's remaining wagon. But Mrs. Wolfinger continued to
cry and beg, until George told our nephews Solomon and William and
their friend John Landrum Murphy to saddle up and go back into the
desert to look for signs of the three men.*

*We waited at the edge of the desert while the sun rose higher, and we
began worrying about the boys too. Around noon, they appeared driving
Mr. Wolfinger's wagon, flushed with heat and self-importance, vying with
each other to get the news out first.*

"We found his wagon and brought it in!"

"It was untouched!"

"Cattle unhitched, standing right next to it!"

"Still chained together!"

"No sign of Wolfinger, boys?" George asked. "Or Spitzer or Reinhardt?"

"Indians must have attacked them," the boys cried.

"Indians don't leave oxen," George said.

*Patrick Breen snorted. "Indians, my foot. Wolfinger was a rich man,
and those other two Dutchmen, I'll stake my life they've seen the inside of
jail more than once—"*

*I doubt that Mrs. Wolfinger could understand Mr. Breen's thick
brogue, but she began sobbing again, and I led her away. "You come with
us. One of our teamsters will drive your wagon."*

Without vote or discussion, the men chained up. We could still get in half a day's travel. We already had lost too much time. No one wanted to go back in that burning desert again. "It's a matter among foreigners," one teamster said, another adding, "Their concern, not ours," and no one disagreed.

Two days later, our fifteen wagons made a meager nooning stop, mostly to rest the jaded teams. We had coffee and tea left. William Eddy held out a small bag of sugar. "This is it for us."

"Hallo!" a voice called.

We stared in disbelief as Mr. Spitzer and Mr. Reinhardt approached our campsite.

"Indians attacked us," Mr. Reinhardt said. "Killed Wolfinger."

"Carried him and his oxen off," Mr. Spitzer said. "Burnt his wagon."

George looked coldly at them. "His wagon and oxen were untouched. We brought them in."

Mr. Reinhardt looked down, but Mr. Spitzer maintained his gaze with George.

Patrick Breen exchanged a look with his wife, Peggy: What did I tell you?

Doris Wolfinger gestured to Mr. Spitzer, whispered to me, "Die Waffe-meines Mannes."

I pointed to the gun at Mr. Spitzer's waist. "She says it's her husband's gun."

George curtly gestured for Mr. Reinhardt and Mr. Spitzer to fall in. I looked at him questioningly. "Write down what everybody says in your journal," he said. "The proper authorities can settle this when we get to California. Right now we need every person we can get."

102 days in the mountains

Sister, there is no way George can relay the children. He keeps talking about it, and his spirits are better, but he has to know his arm is getting worse. We must get out of here, but how? I can't leave him. The children are too little—

I stopped writing there this morning, because George called me. "We'll give the rescuers a few more days," he said. "If they don't come, and the thaw holds, we'll walk out. Jean Baptiste will carry Georgia. I'll carry Eliza. You and Elitha and Leanna will help Frances."

In spite of myself my eyes cut involuntarily to his bandaged arm, and he saw.

"I've got it all worked out," he said. "Milt's going to help us."

I stared at him for a moment, calculating his plan, repeating it in my head and then aloud to hear how it sounded. "Jean Baptiste will carry Georgia. You and Milt will carry Eliza. Elitha and Leanna and I will help Frances."

He nodded.

"George, I think we could do it with Milt."

We looked into each other's eyes, Betsey, and saw hope there. "Yes, yes," I said. "I'm sure we can do it with Milt."

Feb 13th 1847

Much of the morning, George sat at the table instructing Leanna on how to carry his flintlock. "One way's to carry the rifle with your dominant hand, the muzzle forward," he said. "You're right-handed like me, so try that."

Leanna stood next to him, painstakingly following his instructions.

"See how your wrist and forearm are ahead of the lock? That way it can't get accidentally cocked or discharged. But you can also cradle it, if that's more comfortable for you. Your mother and Elitha prefer that."

My father taught me the cradle because, even when I was 10 years old, the gun was more than half as long as I was tall. Elitha was tall for her age but took to the cradle right away. She's an expert shot, but hunted only once because the falling pheasant plunged her heart.

"Now the nice thing about the cradle is that your fingers support the trigger guard bow, and your open hand covers the lock and pan, protecting them."

Leanna carefully shifted the rifle to the cradle position.

"See how the main weight of the rifle's on your left forearm now," George said. "Which one feels better?"

"I want to try both some more," Leanna said.

George nodded approval. "Tomorrow I'll show you how to load it, and then we'll practice shooting."

Leanna beamed—she's younger than Elitha was when she

got that privilege—and shifted from one carry to another a dozen more times.

After so much inactivity, all the movement and talk is thrilling. One more day of preparation, and then Jean Baptiste can fetch Milt.

At the hearth I crisped strips of hide to carry with us, while Elitha lined our dresses and coats with layers of silk for warmth. Next to her, Frances looked dismayed as a steady drip came through a new place in the ceiling. Elitha put her arm around her. "No, it's good, Frances. We want the thaw to continue. We'll be able to leave. Mother and Father told Leanna and me. We have a plan all worked out with Jean Baptiste and Mr. Elliott."

Leanna cradled the rifle again and said, "I think the cradle." She laughed. "Just like a little baby," she said, and Elitha looked over and laughed. We all laughed.

The shelter teems with hope.

15th

*J*ean Baptiste, crying, motioned me outside. He had to tell me twice. I couldn't hear it, couldn't believe it.

I came inside, stood there unsteady on my feet in the smoky dimness. Flames cast shadows on the wall. Dante's Inferno. The only sound was Doris Wolfinger's sobs. I wrenched her blanket back, shook her by the shoulders. "Stop crying!"

She instantly stopped crying and stared at me in panic and fear. I stared furiously at her and left.

"What *is* it?" George said.

I didn't even want to say it aloud. It was terrible to even form the words in a whisper.

"Milt died."

I burst into tears. "Milt died February 9th. Dead all the time we've been making our plan. Margret and Virginia weren't strong enough to bury him. Five days Milt lay dead at the Murphys'. The Breen boys finally went and buried him." I sobbed while George held me.

Milford "Milt" Elliott, 28, d. February 9th 1847 at the lake camp.
   The Reeds' teamster from Springfield. Steadfast and
   brave.

It wasn't until I was recording Milt's death in the Bible that I registered the terrible disappointment on George's face.

15th near midnight

I came back from Elizabeth's near twilight, and George was gone.

I followed his heavy, dragging footprints to just beyond the clearing. His back to me, his gaze was fixed on something in the dim light. He tried to raise his rifle but was too weak. He tried to reposition himself and make another effort.

"George," I said softly.

He turned, hissed. "Quiet. You'll frighten the deer."

My eyes filled with tears.

He made a third herculean effort, bringing the gun above his shoulder, painstakingly lowering it until he had the deer dead in his sights.

And then he saw in the crosshairs what I saw: A tree with hacked branches, moving in the wind.

He turned around, broken. "I'm Hardcoop," he said. He let the gun drop to the snow and walked away.

Taking two steps for every one of his, I struggled after him, screaming at his back. "Hardcoop helped me with the children! He cared for Luke as tenderly as if he were his own grandson! Hardcoop did every single thing he could!"

George stopped, turned. "I'm sorry."

Together, tears streaming down our faces, we wrested the gun from the snow.

Nov 1st 1846

While Elitha and I consoled Georgia and Eliza, Shhh you're okay, the teamsters righted the wagon and hurriedly repacked it. The snowflakes whirling about us, George and Jacob were hastily repairing the broken axle when suddenly Jacob's chisel slipped and gashed George's hand, red blood spurting on white snow. Jacob was beside himself. Oh my God, George, I'm sorry, I'm— I ran to get bandages, and George made light of it, consoling his distraught brother, just for an instant his eyes meeting mine over the deep cut that went diagonally from his wrist across his hand to his little finger, before we cast them down to see the stain spread across the snow.

Truckee Meadows, October 1846
Sister

That is the letter to you I found in the Bible. I can think of many things that would have interrupted me, but not what I intended to tell you.

A salutation when I wrote it, now it looks like a call for help.

Feb 17th 1847

The prairie grass rolls and undulates, rolls and undulates. Elitha looks up from her book and says, "It looks like waves, Mother." "Soon you'll see *real* ocean waves," I say. The prairie grass turns into ocean waves, bigger and bigger waves, spectacular ocean waves turn into waves of blowing snow, blowing higher, higher, until the waves are massive tidal waves just about to drown us all, George goes under first, I reach for Frances, for Eliza, Georgia slips away, I frantically grab Elitha, Leanna's gone, there's no way I can save them all—

"Tamsen, Tamsen," George calls. I open my eyes, stare at him in fright. "What were you dreaming?" he asks. "Nothing," I say. I look at him. "I *believed* it would be advantageous for them." "Of course. Of course," he says, holding my shaking body the rest of the night.

I never went back to sleep. I was afraid to go back to sleep, even shutting my eyes, I saw those terrible waves, the children slipping under, the white, icy fingers of my uncle reaching out to embrace me. I was more tired today than I have ever been, I could hardly force myself to move. Bathing George's wound, my hands shook. *Drip.* No matter how many holes we stuff, Betsey, we always miss some or new ones appear. *Drip.* The single persistent drip hit like a metronome, it pounded in my head. Jean Baptiste and I strung a rope across the shelter to hang the children's clothes on. We stretched out damp clothes on every available surface. I lay stockings across logs by the fireplace. *Drip.* Frances watched the drip with a little smile on her face. No one has told her the plan is off. George's wound has spread farther up his arm. I felt a scream rise up in me and tried to stifle it. *Drip.* I looked up at George, his sad eyes watching me closely.

"The children have not had one dry garment on in more than a week, and I don't know what to do about it. George. We must hold on for the children!"

George reached across the table with his other hand and took mine. "We got through the Wasatch "

I looked into his calm, sad eyes and felt the stillness, the steadiness, at the center of his being flow into me.

"We got through the Wasatch," I said to myself, as I emptied the slops into a trench behind our shelter.

I tossed some snow into the pail, swirled it around, shook it out, and set the pail near the opening. Frances, Georgia, Eliza, and Uno came out, squinting against the brightness of the sunny day. "Told you the sun would come out again," I said. Elitha and Leanna dumped blankets and clothes in a pile on the ground. I waved at Jean Baptiste walking toward us across the clearing. I almost shouted: We got through the Wasatch!

Sweet Frances dug and trudged, helping me pack clean snow into bowls and set them by the shelter. After filling one bowl together, Georgia and Eliza stopped to eat snow and play.

Elitha and Leanna shook a damp blanket to air and smooth it out before laying it on the ground. Jean Baptiste, without a word, took Frances's hand, and they joined the older girls. Each took a corner of the blanket and shook. They've done this often before, but today it turned into a lively team game as each side tried to shake the blanket out of the other side's hands.

Uno rolled in the snow, shaking snow all over, rolling again, Eliza and Georgia laughing at his antics. They were little bundles of dirty, ragged clothes bubbling laughter. Leanna gave a ferocious pull, lost her balance, and in the grabbing and falling, all four ended up falling down, all laughing hard together.

The sun sparkled on the snow. The sky was the bluest you ever saw. I stopped and just looked at the sky. The vastness. The majestic mountains. Sometimes my spirit soars at the boundlessness about us. I lay down in the fresh, clean snow next to Eliza and Georgia and made an angel like you and I used to do so long ago. Eliza and Georgia plopped down next to me and pumped their little angel arms. Then Frances, Leanna, Elitha, even Jean Baptiste did.

Everyone made angels in the snow.

Night

We got through the Wasatch. If I had my oil paints, I'd paint it in crimson. Embroider it on a sampler pillow. We couldn't follow the Weber Canyon route, Betsey, we had to go through the Wasatch Mountains. With axes, hatchets, and sheer brute strength, we went where no wagon had ever gone before, hacking out a road through a labyrinth of forest, thicket, bramble, and underbrush, around and over boulders, fording the same creek thirteen times, often dragging back the pitifully short road to camp at the same spot as the night before, blistering, bleeding, despairing, panicking, it was only with the utmost difficulty that George kept the company together, and after all that, Betsey, for over two weeks and an advance of thirty-six miles, we came to a gorge that was impenetrable.

Nearby was a frighteningly steep hill. There was no way to ascend it—the wagons would roll backward. George went first. We hitched nearly every team of oxen to our lead wagon, and he began the pull up. One slip, and George, forty oxen, and the wagon would have smashed to death.

The wagon over, he brought back the oxen, and the men hitched them to the next wagon. One by one, with mothers and terrified children inside hanging on to canvas sides, wooden frames, and each other, we pulled every one of our wagons, yard by yard, up, and over that precipitous, seemingly perpendicular hill. It was an impossible feat, and only desperation accomplished it.

Tonight as I write down George's words, I'm grateful to be able to record something with full hope, grateful for today.

I was out nearly all day long, this morning with the children, this afternoon at Elizabeth's, then walking by myself until sunset, George's words buoying me all the more because they pulled me up from despair. When I think upon our nearly eight years of marriage, my husband has always been a kind friend, who has done all in his power to promote my happiness. By and large, he has never asked me to be other than I am or less than I am.

Did I tell you, Betsey, that when we married, I told the minister, "In my vow, you must leave out the word *obey*." Immediately, in the most annoying way, he turned to George. George never blinked an eye. The minister waited, as if for permission. "Don't use *obey* in my vow either," George said.

I think we have achieved, as much as possible in an unequal world, a marriage of equals.

June 1846

At our campsite on the Trail, under a dazzling, starry sky, George tucks the children in for the night. "There's nothing like a night under the open stars," he says to them.

"Why aren't you and Momma sleeping out here with us?" Frances asks.

"Old bones," he says.

He climbs into the wagon and winks at me waiting for him in bed. I hold out my arms. Tanned, strong, smiling, he comes to me.

Betsey, last night I lay next to my dear husband. His breathing was labored, he slept fitfully, unaware that he grimaced and moaned from the pain. I thought of all the things that will never again be, allowed myself to cry without sound, and then I put those memories away in the back of my heart.

Feb 18th 1847

"We're on our last hide," I told George.

I read the word on his lips: "Uno."

After the children fell asleep, I beckoned to Jean Baptiste waiting at the fireplace. He picked Uno off the end of the children's platform as gently as lifting a sleeping child.

"Chain up, boys," George says for the first time in our Springfield driveway. "Chain up!"

"Jump, Uno, jump!" Frances yells.

Leanna boosts Uno, and Frances hauls him into the wagon.

Out on the prairie, the girls and I gallop on horses. We ride astride, passing two women riding sidesaddle, who look askance at us. Frances, her arms wrapped around Leanna, shrieks with ecstasy. Barking wildly, Uno tries to keep up. "Uno thinks he's a horse!" Frances screams.

Frances eyed her bits of meat in the watery stew and began eating. Georgia and Eliza gulped theirs down, crying throughout.

"But why did Uno run away?" Eliza sobbed again.

"He ran to California," Frances said, silent tears running down her cheeks.

February 19th 1847 Three months and eighteen days trapped in the mountains

I heard Jean Baptiste at the top of the tree yelling and ran out. "I see them, I see them! Mrs. Donner! They're coming!"

I hurried across the clearing toward the three rescuers on snowshoes. "I am Tamsen Donner," I said. "We have been expecting you."

Mr. Reasin Tucker, about 40, introduced himself and the two others. "Where is Mr. James Reed?" I asked.

"We have not seen him," Mr. Tucker said. "We heard of your distress from William Eddy."

"The snowshoers got through? Thank God."

Mr. Tucker fell silent; the others averted their eyes.

"Please tell me," I said. "How is Mr. Charles Stanton? He was traveling with us. And the other snowshoers?"

Mr. Tucker took my arm and moved with me to the side, lowered his voice.

What he said shook me to my core. When I could speak, I said, "I will get my children ready."

"It's difficult and dangerous, Mrs. Donner. We can only take those who can walk by themselves."

Inside, Doris Wolfinger rushed around frenetically, stuffing things into bundles.

"The snowshoers got through," I said. "Seven men have come. They cannot take everyone today, but another relief will come soon. Elitha, Leanna, we're sending you ahead to get things ready for the family." I pointed to their sisters. Frances was taking in all the stir; Georgia and Eliza halfheartedly played their card game. "It may be that your sisters will arrive at the settlement without Father or me," I said. "God willing, we will follow later. Take good care of them and of yourselves, and always stay together."

I embraced Elitha and Leanna, and they looked at me, their eyes full of tears.

"I don't want to leave you here, Mother," Leanna said. "There's too much work and you'll only have Jean Baptiste to help."

"I have to go, Mother," Elitha said. "I can't bear to stay here another day hearing my little sisters cry for food."

"You both must go to prepare a place for us," I said.

With great effort, George sat in a chair I had padded with blankets. He has so little body fat it's painful for him to sit. Elitha and Leanna knelt in front of him, tears streaming down their faces. "Always honor your mother, Mary Blue, who gave you life," George said. "Honor your mother, Tamsen Donner, who loved and raised you as her own. Do your best in life, and keep me in your hearts." Tears streaming down his face, he embraced them.

All of a sudden, Georgia registered that her big sisters were leaving. She threw herself at Elitha, clinging to her, sobbing, "Don't go without me." With the utmost difficulty, Elitha was able to disengage herself, only by repeatedly promising Georgia, "I will bring you bread." Finally Georgia nodded and, as if she had completely tired herself out, went and climbed onto her rack.

Outside, the three rescuers lined up Elitha, Doris Wolfinger, my nephews, William Hook, and George, and Noah James. "Where's Leanna?" I asked. "She's saying good-bye to Aunt Elizabeth," Elitha said.

Jean Baptiste was distraught. "Why can't I go?" he demanded. "Noah James is going."

Mr. Tucker shook his head no. "Noah's only 16. You have to stay. You're the only able-bodied man left."

Jean Baptiste turned to me. "Please, Mrs. Donner. Let me go with them. I should be allowed to save myself."

"Speak with Mr. Donner," I said.

He raced inside the shelter.

Leanna came across the clearing, her eyes filled with tears. "Thank you, Mother," she said. Her skin was a peculiar sallow color, dry and cold when I touched her cheek. Her once abundant black, wavy hair was coarse and thin. Her body sagged alarmingly as she turned to join the group.

Mr. Tucker parceled out food for those of us staying behind: a teacup of flour, two small biscuits, and thin pieces of jerked beef. I watched with disbelief as he painstakingly measured out the jerked beef, the pieces long as his little finger and half as wide. Each adult ration was as many pieces as he could encircle with his first finger and thumb brought together.

"We're eating our last hide, Mr. Tucker."

"Our supplies were rifled by bears, Mrs. Donner. This is all we can spare."

"If we don't find our cattle in the snow in a day or two, Mr. Tucker . . . we must commence on the dead."

Distress and revulsion crossed all the rescuers' faces.

My voice continued to shake, but I looked them square in the eye. "As long as breath stays in me, I will keep my children alive."

The men looked down at the ground.

They left quickly. Leanna was last in line and almost immediately couldn't keep up. Staggering along in the others' footprints, she fell farther behind. It was as if after holding herself together all these months, she suddenly succumbed to hunger and exhaustion. I had been worrying about the wrong child, I realized. I stood watching her, torn, wanting to run and help her, caught here. Then Elitha turned around, came back, and took Leanna's arm. Leanna leaned heavily upon her, and the two of them made their way together. "They will take care of each other," I whispered. "They will be all right."

Inside, Jean Baptiste, on the brink of tears, said to George, "I lied, Mr. Donner. I'm not twenty-one. I'm only sixteen, just like Noah."

George laid his hand on Jean Baptiste's shoulder. "You must be a man, Jean Baptiste, and do your duty. Care for my children until the next relief comes, and you shall make your home with us forever."

Jean Baptiste snuffled and nodded assent. Silently I let out my breath. I could not have managed without him.

I sat next to George's bed, shaving fat off the pieces of jerked beef. "Elitha, Leanna, Doris Wolfinger, from here. Elizabeth could have gone, but there weren't enough rescuers to carry her children. She sent William Hook and little George. Solomon wanted to go and was furious when Mr. Tucker told him he had to help his mother with the four younger children. Elizabeth said, 'It's William's turn, Solomon.' Jean Baptiste will go over to the lake camp tomorrow to find out who went from there."

George was in his own thoughts, dismayed. "I should have told Elitha and Leanna that sometimes your best is not enough, but you have to do it anyway."

"I think they know that," I said, hoping that they wouldn't have to discover it.

By the fire, Eliza nibbled an inch-long piece of dried beef.

"You'll be sorry if you eat yours all up tonight," Frances warned.

Georgia shook her head. "Elitha's bringing us bread."

"Time to get just a little warm before going to bed," Jean Baptiste said. He raked the coals together as he does many nights, covered them with ashes, and put a large kettle over like a drum.

Georgia and Eliza spread their hands over the kettle. Frances opened her hand, and two gold earrings glittered on her palm. "Mrs. Wolfinger gave them to me when she left," she said.

I looked closely at them. "Real gold," I said. "Tie them in your little kerchief. You may need them someday." I gave the earrings back to Frances, took the pan of beef trimmings, and set it outside to harden into tallow.

Jean Baptiste's Report

FROM THE LAKE CAMP:

Margret Reed, her four children, Virginia, 13, Patty, 9,
James, 6, and Tommy, 4, and Lizzie started out, but Patty
and Tommy had to be brought back. The Breens were
upset but took them in.

Edward, 13, and Simon Breen, 8, went.

Philippine Keseberg carried her little 3-year-old, Ada. Mr.
Keseberg couldn't travel.

The Englishman John Denton, 28, who carved Sarah Keyes's
gravestone.

Our teamster, Noah James, 16.

Three of the Graves children, William, 17, Eleanor, 14, and
Lovina, 12.

Two Murphys, Mary, 14, and William, 10.

A rescuer carried Naomi Pike, 2.

Altogether from both camps, the rescuers took six adults and
seventeen children.

Thirty-two of us are left in the mountains.

Twelve of us here at Alder Creek, twenty at the lake camps.

HERE AT ALDER CREEK:

IN OUR SHELTER

George Donner, 60

Tamsen Donner, 45

Frances Donner, 6

Georgia Donner, 5

Eliza Donner, 3

Also most nights, Jean Baptiste Trudeau, 16

IN ELIZABETH'S SHELTER

Elizabeth Donner, 38

Solomon Hook, 14

Mary Donner, 7

Isaac Donner, 5

Samuel Donner, 4

Lewis Donner, 3

AT THE LAKE CAMP:

IN THE "SHANTY"

Patrick Breen, 51

Margaret Breen, 40

John Breen, 14

Patrick Breen, Jr., 9

James Breen, 5

Peter Breen, 3

Isabella Breen, 1

Also: Martha "Patty" Reed, 9, & Thomas Reed, 4

IN THE MURPHY CABIN AGAINST THE ROCK

Lewis Keseberg moved here

Levinah Murphy, 36

Simon Murphy, 8

Mrs. Murphy's grandchildren, George Foster, 4, Catherine
Pike, 1

Also: William Eddy's son, James Eddy, 3

IN THE DOUBLE CABIN

Elizabeth Graves, 45
Nancy Graves, 9
Jonathan Graves, 7
Franklin Graves, Jr., 5
Elizabeth Graves, 1

Feb 20th 1847

When I came back from Elizabeth's, I saw immediately the cupboard door was open. My heart plummeted.

I didn't even need to look inside for those meager rations I planned to parcel out until the next rescue.

The children had eaten every last scrap.

I didn't trust myself to say anything, although Frances hid under her cover half the day. When I was composed enough, I drew the cover back. Her face was tearstained, and fear and sorrow were in her eyes. "I told Georgia and Eliza no, I told them—" She began crying again and blurted out, "I ate some too, Mother."

"Of course you did," I said. "You're hungry, Frances. It's okay. It's okay."

All we have now is the pan of tallow I cut into squares.

I instructed Jean Baptiste to take Frances, Georgia, and Eliza outside and march them around the clearing. "No matter the weather, you must take them twice a day," I told him.

I was equally stern with the children. "You must learn to keep your balance on the slick, frozen parts," I said. "You must know how to wade through drifts and slush. Rescue is coming soon, and you must be ready."

While they were outside, I bathed George's arm. As I swished the cloth in warm water, there was a little *ping*. My wedding ring had slid off and hit the bottom of the pan. I quickly fished it out and put it in my pocket, but George saw. I continued to bathe his arm. The infection has spread to his shoulder.

"It took the snowshoers thirty-two days to reach the first settlement," I said. "Of the fifteen who went, seven survived. Two of the men and all five women. Charles Stanton died. Dear Mr. Stanton—"

I was too choked up to go on. George put his other hand on mine. "Stanton was a brave man," he said. "Twice he went ahead to help us. Many men would have kept going, but he came back each time. Once he was over the mountains and all the way to Sutter's Fort and he came back to help us, even though he had no family here."

The Bible was open to **Deaths** on the table beside us, and I stared at what I had recorded:

Charles Stanton, 35, d. Dec ? 1846 en route in mtns. with the snowshoe party. From the storehouse of his honor, he enriched our Company.

Patrick Dolan, 35? d. Dec ? 1846 en route in mtns. with the snowshoers

Franklin Graves, 57, d. Dec 25 1846 en route in mtns. with the snowshoers

Lemuel Murphy, 12, d. Dec ? 1846 en route in mtns. with the snowshoers

Antonio(?) 23? d. Dec ? 1846 en route in mtns. with the snowshoers

Jay Fosdick, 23, d. Jan ? 1847 en route in mtns. with the snowshoers

Luis and Salvador, d. Jan ? 1847, the Indians from Sutter's Fort, ages unknown, en route in mtns. with the snowshoers. Murdered.

I looked at George and my voice cracked, but I finally got it out. "Most of those who perished gave their bodies so that others might live."

"No," George said.

"As might we——" I began.

George struggled to get up. "I'll find the cattle under the snow."

"Wait till I bandage your arm," I said.

"How could I do this to you and the children? How could I——"

I stared at him, suddenly flooded with fury. "I wanted this as much as you did," I said. "I wanted this *more* than you did. For better and for worse, George Donner, we did this together!"

Spring 1846

$\mathcal{G}$eorge's eyes and mine were wet, and Elitha was sobbing, when we drew away from our home in Springfield, but once the die was cast, we all turned our eyes to the future. Those first six weeks were filled with excitement and happiness and hope. Every day the weather grew finer, the sky bluer, the sun sparkling off our gleaming white wagon covers, our lead yokes Brindle and Bright, Old Sock and Blue, and the other oxen yokes effortlessly pulling along our mighty wagons, at night we danced and sang, and each day we joined more wagons coming from every direction, all of us racing to Independence to meet our destiny. Even Sarah Keyes's death, though sad, seemed a natural part of the order of things.

Did I write you about her burial, Betsey? I think about all the burials so often I can't remember if I wrote you or just talked about them with you in my head. No matter.

Our first burial

Sarah Keyes was our first death. You remember I told you she wouldn't be parted from Margret Reed, her only daughter? She was 70 and an invalid, and the stay-at-home gossips had a field day with that. "Dragging that poor old lady into the wilderness. It's a sin. James Reed thinks he can defy nature itself."

If there were hushed conferences inside the Reeds' house, Sarah Keyes's wishes were ultimately deferred to, and James had his furniture factory build a special wagon to make his mother-in-law as comfortable as possible. A double-decker with a level raised for her bed, spring seats, a tiny sheet-metal stove vented through the top. Oh my, Elizabeth coveted that stove.

"They've never seen a wagon like this crossing the plains," James said, and George said, "I think you can safely say that, James."

The big wagon, built to ease and pleasure an old woman, was so relatively grand it caused resentment almost from the beginning and, though people would probably deny it, certainly played a part in James's banishment from the train—leaving Margret and the children behind to abandon the wagon and most of their possessions in the second desert. But on the April morning we left Springfield, cached wagons and banishment undreamed of, her sons carried Sarah Keyes out of the house and placed her in the gleaming wagon on a large feather bed, propping her up with pillows. One last time they implored her to reconsider. They knew and she knew that it was the last time they would see each other. Sarah Keyes's eyes were full of tears as we drove out of Springfield, and she had her little granddaughter hold up the wagon cover to have a last look at her old home, the way I turned around from the front seat of our wagon to have a last look at ours.

Springfield, Illinois, to Alcove Springs, Kansas. 470 miles. Sarah Keyes had less than six weeks with her daughter, but I think if she had had that knowledge before she left, she would have made the same decision. That May day, our first death, was sad, but Sarah Keyes was old, and her time, perhaps hastened a bit, was near. A baby, Lewis Keseberg, Jr., was born the same day she died, reminding us of the cycle of endings and beginnings, tempering our grief with hope. No one dreamed that death was rushing to greet so many in that crowd of mourners. "It seemed hard to bury her in the wilderness and travel on," Margret told me later, "but Momma's death there, before our troubles began, was providential, and nowhere on the whole road could we have found so beautiful a resting place." All the emigrants turned out to assist at the funeral; the men hewed a coffin out of a cottonwood tree; a minister said words; a young Englishman, John Denton, chiseled SARAH KEYES BORN IN VIRGINIA and her dates on a large, gray stone. She was buried under the shade of an oak, the stone placed at the foot of the grave, and Charles Stanton, the children, and I planted wildflowers in the sod.

Not nine months hence, Mr. Tucker told me that on their way coming in to rescue us, they passed Charles Stanton, frozen to death alone in the snow with no one to mark the passing or bury the body.

But on May 26, 1846, there was still time for ceremony, and Sarah Keyes, surrounded by family, friends, and members of our company paying our respects, was laid to rest by the Big Blue River.

Sarah Keyes, 70, d. May 26th 1846 at Alcove Springs, Kansas. Margret Reed's mother. Peacefully of old age, her daughter, son-in-law, and grandchildren around her.

Catherine Pike, 1, d. Feb 20th 1847 at the lake camp

I carefully cut a piece from the bolt of red velvet and made a ribbon to wear my wedding ring around my neck. No one mentioned it, and I thought it just as well they hadn't noticed.

A little while ago, George reached across the table and traced the ribbon with his index finger down to the gold ring, circled it, and smiled at me. The most tender, bittersweet smile. My eyes welled, I had to turn away.

March 1846, Springfield

In our farmhouse, it's nighttime. Supper and dishes are done, but it's not yet bedtime. A fire is burning, the lamps are lit. Everything seems to glow, bathed in an almost golden light. Leanna threads the drawstring through a leather bag she has made for her best marbles. George rough-houses with Georgia and Eliza, tossing them into the air, each shrieking and begging for another turn. Before dinner Frances and Leanna mischievously braided his hair into a score of tiny little black braids shot with silver that, to the girls' delight, he wore all through supper and hasn't taken out yet, really how could one not love a man like that? Elitha, by the fire, is buried in her Dickens, oblivious to all the happy noise. Near the table where men's, women's, and children's clothes in various stages of completion are laid out, Frances stands on a hassock and fidgets in a half-made dress. I sit on the floor, pins in my mouth, pinning Frances's hem. "The trip will take five to six months," I say, "so we'll leave a deep hem for growing."

Today, eleven months later, I let out the last of the hem and Frances's little spindly shanks were still exposed. She has grown like a weed, but only vertically. I looked at this child forced to endure so much beyond her six years, and I thought my heart would break.

"You're going to be tall like your father," I said.

Our Second Burial, Luke Halloran

The morning after the men voted to take Hastings Cutoff, all was chaos and confusion at the "Parting of the Ways," as the majority of wagons lined up to take the regular route and our nineteen wagons lined up separately to take the Cutoff. At the campfire, I was nearly scouring the finish off the coffeepot with sand when Luke Halloran said earnestly to George, "I have money, sir."

"It's not a question of money, son," George said. "I'm sorry."

"Please, Mr. Donner," Luke said.

George shook his head and turned away. Kneeling next to me, he whispered, "Thrown out of his wagon. T.B.," he mouthed.

I watched the dejected young man, and for an instant I was back in North Carolina, bent over Tully, feverish on his bed, a Christmas tree nearby.

"We can put Mr. Halloran in the third wagon," I said.

"The children——," George began.

"I'll keep the children away," I said.

And when George still hesitated, I spit out, "That boy is sick and totally alone in the world. He needs to get to California fast. He needs a shortcut far more than any of us do."

George and I locked gaze a moment, then he got up. "Halloran," he called. Luke turned around, and George nodded. Luke's face became ecstatic.

Day after day, trying to outrun his sickness, trying to hold on until the famed California sun could heal his poor lungs, Luke grew weaker. He was an object of pity at first, until the men turned mean in the Wasatch, and stood outside our wagon yelling at him and Hardcoop, "Get out here now, shirkers!" I opened the wagon cover, looked at their faces contorted with rage. "Are you mad?" I said. "No, they're right, Mrs. Donner," Luke said from behind me, and he and old Hardcoop staggered out. Time and again over those endless hills, Luke climbed out, stood there racked with consumption, trying to help as much as he could with the unloading, the pulling of the ropes, everything he did not enough and hastening his own decline.

On August 29th, George pulled the oxen out of line so Luke could die without jars and lurches. His head lay in my lap; his face, just into manhood, flushed red in a mockery of good health. I stroked his hair, trying to soothe him. He never took his eyes off mine, until shade by shade, barely perceptible, the light went out of them.

That night, we came into camp with the body. "He came from County Galway, Ireland," I said. "He opened a general store in St. Joseph, Missouri. His health was good until three months ago."

George opened a letter and read, "I bequeath everything to George and Tamsen Donner, who took me in."

James Reed wasn't the only one who smiled slightly.

When George opened the battered trunk, stenciled LUKE HALLORAN, I heard a long, low whistle behind me. Much to everyone's amazement, including ours, we saw $1,500.00 in silver coin and full Mason regalia.

"One of your fraternal brothers, James," George said.

"I'll conduct the funeral according to the Masonic ritual," James said.

The next day on the white alkali salt flats in the wilderness, the men dug a grave next to a fresh mound—JOHN HARGRAVE tarred on a wooden board—from Hastings Company, which we were trying to catch up with. "Well, at least we know that Hastings exists," Patrick Breen said.

We wrapped Luke Halloran, 25 years old, in clean sheets and a buffalo robe, and the men proceeded to lay him to rest in a bed of almost pure salt.

"Isn't anybody going to make him a coffin?" I asked.

"He's already delayed us too much," muttered a teamster, and another said, "We shouldn't have stopped at all."

"The day we don't stop to bury our dead will be a sorry day for us," George said.

"Don't worry, Mrs. Donner," Patrick Breen said. "That's almost pure salt. Those bodies will still be preserved on Judgment Day."

Even though the "dry drive" was still ahead, we gave Luke Halloran a full day. Now when we look back and see that that full day might have gotten us over the mountain pass before the snow made it impossible, it's hard to understand that so few of us objected to taking the time.

Still . . . With all our troubles, this was our first death since Sarah Keyes in Alcove Springs. Luke had been in our wagon, and George was the Captain. We had made it through the Wasatch and welcomed a rest. I'm sure I wasn't the only one shaken by the bitter quarreling in the Wasatch. A burial similar to one at home would be proof that we were the same people who had started out, good people, our values intact. James Reed, a Mason, officiated at the full Masonic funeral he would want for himself.

Now I think we were all whistling in the dark.

I did not yet know that a death, noticed and special, would one day strike me as a triumph.

Luke Halloran, 25, d. Aug 25th 1846 on the south side of Salt Lake, of tuberculosis, traveling in our wagon from Little Sandy, the "Parting of the Ways."

Feb 24th 1847

*O*ut of the corner of my eye today, I saw a shape move behind the trees.

I stopped.

It stopped.

I stood still for a long time. I could see something there motionless.

Then the shape moved in front of the tree. It was an Indian.

I walked to the line of trees. Our eyes met. He held out his hand and gave me two large acorns.

He vanished so swiftly that were it not for the acorns in my hand I would have thought I imagined him.

I boiled the acorns until I could crack them with a rock, then boiled them again for hours to take the bitterness out. I pounded them into a mash for the three littlest children. Georgia and Eliza gobbled theirs. Frances let her tiny bit lie in her mouth until it dissolved into nothing.

His face was so sorrowful it seemed to me that he knew of our suffering. His sympathy seemed as much of a gift as the acorns, and it comforted me.

Our Third Burial

$\mathcal{G}$eorge and I were two days ahead so we weren't witness to our third death, John Snyder, nor his burial, "wrapped in a shroud, a board below, a board above," James Reed told us.

John Snyder. That handsome young man full of charm and confidence and life waiting to be grabbed.

I remember well the day I met him, Betsey.

August 10th 1846, the Graves Family join us. The Donner Party is now eighty-six.

On the third day waiting by the Weber River for Mr. Reed, Mr. Stanton, and Mr. Pike to come back with Lansford Hastings to lead us, nerves raw and fear building, the campfire deserted, we heard a clatter, everyone instantly appearing from their wagons to watch—unbelieving—three wagons tear down the hacked out trail toward us with whoops and shouts.

"Hallo! I'm Franklin Graves, Sr., from Illinois. We started out for Oregon but changed our minds. We heard about you at Fort Bridger and came to join up." He waved a hand at his wife and the raucous group tumbling out behind her. "This is my wife, Elizabeth, our eight unmarried children, our newlyweds, and our teamster, the finest on the road. Thirteen in all, and a luckier bunch you'll never meet." The newlyweds held hands, the bridegroom carrying a violin in his other hand.

How the merry, boisterous group distracted us from our fears and raised our spirits.

"Come with me," I said, "I'll write down your names."

The teamster jumped down, removed his hat with a flourish, and bowed to me. "John Snyder, 25, Driver par Excellence, at your service, ma'am."

John Snyder, 25, d. Oct. 5th 1846 in Nevada territory. The Graveses' teamster, "Driver par Excellence," accidentally killed by James Reed.

When Jean Baptiste finishes marching Frances, Georgia, and Eliza around the clearing, I sit them on a log and, like times tables twice a day, I drill:

"What lies beyond those snowy peaks?"

"California."

"Go on."

"There we will be safe, and have food, and our sisters are waiting for us."

"If Father or I are not with you, what do you say when people ask who you are?"

"We are the children of George and Tamsen Donner."

"Eliza, I can't hear you."

"We are the children of George and Tamsen Donner."

"Very good."

Later on, it seemed so clear that we should have gone back and wintered in Truckee Meadows. But then, to go back nearly fifty miles, to slog through that newly fallen snow, George's hand bleeding through the bandages, the oxen barely able to drag themselves along, our wagons rickety and in tatters, to turn back after all the wandering and the quarrels and the deaths, would have been to admit no miracle was going to happen, to admit that we were not going to reach California this year. I can write it even simpler: We could not bear to go back.

"*Well-seasoned wood and flawless,*" *George says.* "*We don't want to break an axle a thousand miles out.*"

A cascade of coffee beans pouring into coarse sacks. Sugar pouring, "*we're taking ten pounds apiece,*" *Elizabeth says,* "*take twenty, I say, take salt, and cornmeal, and baking soda, and rice and beans and bacon and lard and spices and dried fruit and a keg of pickles . . .*"

"*We can count on antelope and buffalo,*" *George says.*

Elitha sits at a barrel with a pad and pencil. The other children help me scoop and ladle flour into large burlap sacks. "*If we take a hundred and fifty pounds of flour for each adult, half ration for children,*" *I ask,* "*how many pounds will we need?*"

"*Do Leanna and I count as adults or children?*" *Elitha asks.*

"*You barely eat, but count both of you as adults,*" *I say.*

Elitha figures madly. Leanna, who has marshaled Frances and Georgia into a team and challenged me to a race—Who can fill a sack the fastest?—scoops faster than I do. Eliza covers her face with flour. "*Eliza's a ghost,*" *Frances says, laughing wildly.*

Respectable people with duties, we bore our obligations in mind, Betsey, and made solid plans.

Feb 25th 1847

Today, Frances, Georgia, and Eliza sprawled limply on their platforms, looking so much like my niece Mary and my nephews across the clearing it gave me a start. I cut three tiny squares of tallow, the last in the pan, and gave them each one. Without getting up, Georgia and Eliza ate theirs in one gulp. Frances sat up, nibbled the tiniest crumb from hers, wrapped the rest in a little cloth, put it in her pocket, and lay back down.

Jean Baptiste scraped the last scrap of the last hide.

"Girls, Jean Baptiste is nearly finished," I said. "Get ready to go outside."

Nobody moved.

"Frances."

"Don't want to." Frances started crying.

She has not cried once, and I had to tell her, "Frances, please don't cry. I need you to help me with your sisters. I'll get you some water, but then you must go out. You must be ready for the rescuers."

I turned to ladle water and suddenly realized the fire rug, a partial hide that catches the sparks, had nearly disappeared. "What happened to the fire rug?" I asked. I bent to examine it, turned back to the children. Frances's face was so guilty, I knew immediately. "You ate it, didn't you?" I said. "You're very clever girls."

Frances stopped crying and smiled in relief. "We cut it in little teeny pieces and toasted them," she said. "They were very tasty. We ate Georgia's doll too."

I thought my heart was beyond breaking. I put another log on the fire, took the last strips of hide, and put them in the pot to boil.

"When is Elitha bringing my bread?" Georgia whined for the hundredth time.

May 12th 1846

Leaving Independence, Missouri, the "jumping-off place," as our wagon passed the American Tract Society, a missionary reached up and handed pamphlets and a Bible to the children. "Give the tracts and Bible to the heathens," he said.

"What are heathens, Mother?" Frances asked.

"They mean the Indians," Elitha said, when I didn't answer.

"And anyone else who has a thought different from them," I said.

June 1846

At daybreak at our campsite on the Plains, Frances in her nightgown went out of our tent pitched at the end of the wagon train. She rubbed her eyes, headed for a tree, saw two Indians watching her, and turned around running for her life. Big-eyed, scared witless, she burst into the tent, yelling, "The heathens, Momma!"

Everybody tensed. George reached for a pistol, I got the rifle. George, his hand on the pistol in his leather vest pocket, went outside. I watched through the tent flap, my rifle ready.

The Indians, one young, one older, perhaps father and son, looked at George solemnly.

George stood very still.

Suddenly the older one smiled and handed George a freshly killed rabbit.

George turned around and called, "We're having guests for breakfast."

I put the rifle down.

George, the five girls, the two Indians, and I having breakfast in our *tent was more than friendly, Betsey, it was antic. They examined the presents with delight, stacking the bolts of bright cotton, beads, and a spyglass next to them.*

The younger Indian, fascinated by Grandmother's hand mirror, could not stop admiring his countenance. Both he and the older Indian wore ornaments tastefully arranged, consisting of beads, feathers, and a fine shell, various colored bark, and the hair from the scalps they have taken in battle.

The older Indian pointed to the mirror and said, "Solid water." Then he hit his chest, and said, "Chief."

George and I nodded vigorously.

He pointed to the young Indian, and said, "Chief."

We again nodded vigorously.

He pointed to George and said, "Chief."

"Well, in our country, we're all chiefs——" George began.

The young Indian cut George off, hit his own chest, "Chief," pointed to the older Chief, and the round began again, the chiefing and nodding continuing until little Eliza hit her chest and piped up, "Chief." Everybody laughed, and Eliza was so pleased she did it again, and then the younger Chief held up the mirror and pointed to his image, "Chief."

Frances whispered to me, "Shall we give them the Bible?"

"They have their own religion," I said. "They don't need ours."

Feb 25th 1847, evening

I sliced the Bible's leather cover into strips and crisped them on the fire. They provided us sustenance.

The minute Jean Baptiste left with the children, George said, "I want you to write something down in your journal."

He waited until I got my pen, then he dictated:

"This great move west could not be stopped. If soldiers stood on the prairie with cannons, they could not have stopped it. It is too big, too deep. Its time has come. Yearning has met with opportunity."

He looked at me and added, "If you and I had not come, it would not have affected the Great Migration one iota. It would only have affected us."

Then he got up from the table and lay down on his platform.

Did he mean we wouldn't be here starving? Or did he mean we would have missed being a part of it? Even if I weren't afraid to ask him the question that fills my mind, the solemnity and urgency of his tone forestalled any question or comment.

*Y*esterday and the day before we had nothing but water.

Last night I turned the page of my journal, and there was a dried flower. "To preserve their form and color, Tamsen," my stepmother said, "specimens collected in the field are spread flat on newspaper and dried between blotters." I idly picked the flower up; it was tiny and delicate and had retained its bright purple color.

"Look at this, children," I said, mainly to distract them from hunger. "Do you remember? Out on the prairie?"

Out on the prairie on a golden summer day, Charles Stanton botanizes with Frances, Georgia, and Eliza, and my niece Mary. They turn over stones, scrape out crevices, gather moss, roots, and flowering plants. Nearby, I kneel close to a tiny purple wildflower, sketching it, then I press it on my journal page. I hear Mr. Stanton say, "Look, children, it's the lupine! Go show your mother." I look up as sun-browned Frances and Georgia run to me, their chubby fists stuffed with purple lupine. Their little legs seem to pump in slow motion as if the shimmering day will go on forever.

I turned the pages of my journal for the children, showing them the pressed form or watercolor sketch of each flower. The vivid

Skewy Delphinium

colors contrasted cruelly with the girls' pallor and our stark surroundings. "Remember, we found the wild tulip," I said. "The primrose."

Frances pointed to one and said, "Mr. Stanton found the lupine."

"That's right," I said. "Here's the eardrop. The larkspur. This, why this one is edible, and so is this—" My fingers trembling, I peeled the dried flower off the page and put it on Frances's tongue like communion.

"Look, Mother," Georgia said. "It left its shadow on the page."

She and Eliza stuck out their tongues for their flowers.

Our Fourth Burial

*H*ardcoop's body was left to be rifled by Indians or animals or both, his bones bleaching in the sun.

> **Hardcoop, 60?, d. Oct 7–8th? 1846** in the desert. Originally from Belgium, one daughter there, name unknown. Abandoned.

Mr. Wolfinger's body had to meet a similar fate.

> **Mr. Wolfinger, 22–26?, d. Oct ? 1846** between Humboldt Sink and Truckee River. Disappeared. Foul play suspected. From Germany, husband of Doris.

William Pike, our sixth death, was our fourth burial.

It was our second day in Truckee Meadows, our eyes darting to the snowy mountaintops above, as we rested the jaded oxen for the long pull up. A gray day, we were awakened with honks. "Geese," George said, springing up before he remembered that his shooting arm was out of commission.

Lewis Keseberg heard the honks too, slipped on the soft moccasins Philippine had traded a silver pitcher for at Fort Bridger, hurried quickly across the ground, suddenly felled by pain as a charred willow stub pierced his heel.

"Bad luck," Lewis Keseberg was saying again to Philippine and me as I cut out the stub when we heard a commotion outside.

George came in just as we finished bandaging Lewis's heel. "There's been a bad accident. William Pike's dying."

William Pike was with the Murphy clan, Levinah Murphy's son-in-law, Harriet's husband, Naomi and Catherine's father. At the Weber River, he had volunteered with Charles Stanton and James Reed to go after Lansford Hastings. He was rarely seen without Mrs. Murphy's other son-in-law, William Foster. Foster and Pike, Pike and Foster: we often said one name with the other. So like brothers were they, always joking and joshing in shorthand, good-naturedly competing in even the tiniest task, their wives joked they had a hard time telling them apart.

At the campfire, William Pike was cleaning a pepperbox rifle, William Foster next to him, saying, "You're not doing that right, Will, I better show you how."

"We need some wood, boys," Mrs. Murphy said.

Pike got up, handed the rifle to Foster, said, "Try to do a better job than you usually do," and turned to get wood. The rifle discharged, striking Pike in the back. He died after a half hour of terrible suffering.

No coffin, no boards for William Pike, there were none to spare. There were no buffalo robes, sheets, blankets, tarps. The men could barely scrape out a depression in the hard ground. All the Murphys dazed, Foster sobbing, Pike's little daughters trying to hug their father, George said a prayer and we laid Pike in a hole barely deep enough to contain him.

From Sarah Keyes's casket lovingly hewed from a cottonwood tree, carved stone, wildflowers planted in the sod, to this in five months.

William Pike, 32, d. Oct 26th 1846 in Truckee Meadows. Husband and father, Levinah Murphy's son-in-law, traveling with the Murphy clan. Accidentally killed by his brother-in-law.

*A*ll that just to get us here. All that grief and confusion and chicanery and betrayal and carelessness and death just to get us here to these dull, thudding, stuporous, barely noticeable deaths. Our teamsters lay in their shelter deathlike, and when life left there was hardly a difference. Mrs. Wolfinger might as well have been a ghost for all the life she brought us.

All of this we bring with us. "We will carve out a new country," we shouted, not realizing that the new country will be no more and no less than the worst and the best of us.

I log deaths. Accidents. When death stalks, do some people go out to meet it? Why do some people lie down and die? How far can a person be pushed until she stops caring about others? I am a schoolteacher doing life and death sums.

When I used all the pages and the end flaps, I went back and found many spaces I had squandered on earlier entries. You can write a whole book in the margins, Betsey. After I carefully cut my journal's leather cover into strips, its linen underflaps yielded me a vast expanse if I wrote very, very small. I thought it would give me a pang to cut my journal cover, I held off all this time, but it was easy after the Bible. I carefully slit the binding threads. Set the pages aside. Sliced the leather cover into strips. I was so excited when I discovered I could turn my journal ninety degrees and write in between the lines of earlier entries. I trust you can read it, Betsey. I know I should put dates. The days are so alike it is easy to lose track. I try to insist the children mark the calendar, but it is a willed action. I don't care. If I wanted to find out something, I could figure it out from the calendars. Why would I want to? During the day I keep us all moving on a narrow path, one step at a time, with the possibility at any moment of someone plunging over. It consumes all my energy to keep them, to keep myself, from looking down into the abyss. Sometimes I think I cannot get through one more day. The thought of my waiting journal keeps me going through the cold and the dark. To let go of time and season and place is exquisite freedom for me. I have never known such freedom. The abyss is still out there, but I pick up my pen and like Icarus I soar.

$\mathcal{A}$nd then another day passed with nothing but water.

I couldn't coax or prod the children to get up.

Eliza looked at me, her eyes great in her thin face. "I want another flower, Momma."

"There are no more, Eliza," I said. "I'm so sorry."

She kept looking at me, pleading wrestling with sadness in her face, then she closed her eyes.

I felt something in my heart turn to steel. "Sleep, my little baby," I said. "Rescue is coming soon."

*O*ne little scrap of the blue calico I had tied on the pole whipped in the wind like a flag shred. Jean Baptiste pulled the pole out of the snow and laid it on the ground.

He and I dug until we reached a body wrapped in a quilt.

"You carry Mr. Shoemaker to the trees," I said. "I will come as soon as everyone is asleep."

*W*hen I was certain everyone was sleeping, I slipped on my cloak and started to leave.

"Tamsen," George whispered, startling me. I turned around. "If anyone wakes," he said, "I will keep them inside."

I was walking into abomination, and he was at my side walking with me.

Jean Baptiste was waiting by the tree. We built a small fire and, in its shadows, knelt over the figure on the ground.

I unwrapped the quilt. Jean Baptiste gasped, looked as if he might falter.

"He is dead, Jean Baptiste. We are alive."

For a long, silent moment, I looked at the body, not sure if I was gathering my strength or praying or both.

"But, Mrs. Donner," Jean Baptiste said, "if we take part of his body, his spirit will never rest."

"God will help him and us, Jean Baptiste." I leaned down and said, "Thank you, Samuel."

With one stroke of the cleaver, I cleaved the breastbone.

Removed the heart and lungs.

I set down bowls of stew, and Georgia and Eliza gobbled.

Frances looked at the chunks of meat suspiciously and then at me.

I looked steadily back at her. If she asked, I planned to tell her Jean Baptiste had found an ox in the snow.

She took a spoonful and broke the gaze, and her eyes went blank. She continued to spoon stew into her mouth mechanically, her arm completely detached from wherever she had gone.

I offered George a bowl. He shook his head. "Save it for the children," he said, tears rolling down his cheeks before he turned his face away.

Dry-eyed, I ate a bowl of gluey ox hide, remembering the December night when Joseph Reinhardt staggered into our shelter and said he was going to Hell.

We're already in Hell.

"*Guess what I cooked today,*" *Elizabeth asked when we pushed open her kitchen door, a streak of flour on her plump cheek, turning back to her oven, without a question or how do you do about the mail-order parcels filling our arms, though our niece and nephews were nearly knocking us over with yells and hugs, barely able to contain themselves until I started untying string. Elizabeth set six steaming pies on a rack, wiped her hands on her apron, cut George half a pie, and said, "Last summer's berries. I experimented with drying them . . ."*

"*Guess what I cooked today,*" *Elizabeth called to me from her wagon as I made my way to the prairie to botanize and sketch some new specimens. "You know those wild peas you and Mr. Stanton found? Leanna helped me make pickled peas! I saved you a bite. Jacob and the boys just gobbled them down. I said, 'These are a delicacy.' Might as well talk to the cat. They don't care what I make as long as there's enough of it.*"

"Guess what I cooked today," Elizabeth asked me this evening in a tone on the edge of hysteria, and then answered the question herself in the same bright shrill tone. "Shoemaker's arm."

She burst into tears.

Dry-eyed, I rocked her. "Shhh. Shhh. It's the right thing you're doing."

"Do you really think so, Tamsen?" she asked, her eyes wide, as trusting as a child.

"I am certain," I said and felt her body relax in my arms.

And I am certain. I also feel that something inside of me has changed irrevocably and I will never cry again.

$\mathcal{A}$nd now the great violation is done once, twice, and as many more times as needed, and all I feel is deep relief that the children are visibly stronger and an equally deep anger.

But anger at whom? Or what?

Not God. I used to feel confident and buoyed that God was guiding my every step, but now I falter too much for that to be true. I don't think God is thinking about us, Betsey. Does that shock you? At first I prayed a great deal, and though I still pray, it seems clear to me that our hope lies in ourselves and each other.

Not George, though I flooded with anger when he said, How could I do this to you and the children? Of all the things men have kept from women, I have always chafed at their robbing us of the joy and risk of adventure, and for an instant, I actually felt like striking him. But that passed as quickly as it had arisen. George is the most equitable man I have ever met—though sometimes it seems to me that a man who simply acts like a decent human being gets undue praise. I leave it on record that this adventure has gone more horribly wrong than anyone could ever have imagined, and I bear equal blame, as I would have deserved equal credit had it gone right.

Am I just railing at life? Bad fortune? Although I have not eaten human flesh, I feel I've become a wild thing. If I looked into Grandmother's mirror, I would see blood dripping from my sharp teeth.

Maybe it would be better if I didn't write my feelings down. The night we couldn't get wood for two days and the fire went out and the cold went to our very marrow and the darkness seemed absolute, I scribbled all night long thinking, If I put down my pen, I will start screaming and never stop. Whenever my mind gets close to that place, I wrench it away. I don't ever want to go there again.

Did I tell you that when Jean Baptiste came through the door with wood in his arms, we all sobbed as if he were carrying a newborn baby?

I cannot tell you how deep is my wish to share our experience here with you. With anyone outside these walls of snow. It's more than a wish. It's a compulsion. We may die here, Betsey.

My whole life my heart was big with hope and impatient with desire. When anyone ever went anyplace, I always wondered: What will they see? What is there that is not here? What waits for them that I am missing?

I cannot bear it if no one knows what has gone on here. What I have seen. What was waiting for me here that I have not missed.

March

1847

March 1st morning

I had a peculiar dream last night, Betsey. I was sailing along the water in the most tranquil way. I had been aboard a great sailing ship and gradually realized that I was now on a smaller boat much closer to the sea—perhaps a tender that the ship had provided for us. I lay in a cunning space, in bed but not asleep, this small boat gently bobbing along, rocking me, the water's surface calm and serene. I looked over and saw George was next to me, though we didn't talk or touch, the current bearing us along together. I cannot emphasize too much how peaceful it was.

I thought of the baby Moses sailing down the stream.

Occasionally I wondered, Am I on the great sailing ship? No, I would realize, I'm in this smaller conveyance, close to but not on the great ship. Even after I woke up, this was the first thing I wondered, until I realized I lay on my rack in the dark and everyone else was still asleep.

I lay there thinking about the dream, and after some time it came to me that those small cunning spaces George and I lay in were sarcophagi.

Was my body having a presentiment of my death? I thought almost in detachment.

It was only later that day that I remembered from my Greek that *sarcophagus* means flesh-eating.

*March 2nd 1847, four months trapped
in the mountains*

The second relief came today.

James Reed came back, I knew he would if he were alive.

James Reed and three other rescuers started into Elizabeth's
shelter and recoiled. They tied scarves over their mouths and
went in. Two came out and vomited in the snow. "Burn it,"
James said. "Build them a new one."

I saw James pull the scarf off his mouth and take a deep
breath before he entered our shelter.

When I came in, he was bent near George's face, speaking
quietly. George looked at me. "Take the children and go with
James. He says Commander Woodworth is due in a week with a
large rescue party. I'll go with them."

"We'll go together then," I said.

James's gaze burned into me, and I looked back steadily until
he broke the gaze.

James had tears in his eyes as he clasped George's good arm.
"Good-bye, old friend," he said. "I hope to see you in California."

George's eyes were wet too. "Don't they call California Para-
dise, James?"

Outside, James put his hand on my arm and spoke with urgency. "George will never reach the settlements."

"I'll get my niece and nephews dressed for travel," I said.

I hurried the three children out of the new tent the men had erected for Elizabeth, the old one still burning nearby.

"I'm leaving Cady and Clark here, Stone at the lake camp," James said. "One man for each tent to cook and as fast as possible resuscitate the enfeebled, so they might start in a few days with the Third Relief."

"We'll be ready," I said.

There are fourteen of us left in the mountains, five at the lake, nine here.

OUR SHELTER:
George Donner
Tamsen Donner
Frances Donner
Georgia Donner
Eliza Donner
Jean Baptiste Trudeau

ELIZABETH'S SHELTER:
Elizabeth Donner
Samuel Donner, 4
Lewis Donner, 3

LAKE CAMP: MOVED INTO THE "SHANTY"
Lewis Keseberg
Levinah Murphy
Simon Murphy, 8
George Foster, 4
James Eddy, 3

*W*henever I went to Elizabeth's, the smell of sickness and un-washed bodies lying in their own waste hit me like a slap, but I thought that my tedious insistence that the children wash their faces daily in a bowl of melted snow, my emptying the slop pots daily, weather permitting, had kept our shelter well, it would be laughable to say orderly or clean, but given the circumstances, as clean as possible. Early on, I do recall wanting to get the children outside, away from the smell of unwashed bodies and sickness, but at some point I began thinking of us not like beasts as Elitha said but like bears burrowed in layers of smudged dirt, waiting for spring. It wasn't until I saw James pause outside our shelter, pull the scarf off his face, and breathe deeply before he entered, that I realized our airless shelter must also smell disgusting. I suppose one can get accustomed to anything. I also realized that I have underestimated James's sensitivity to George's and my feelings. Or perhaps he has changed too.

We all came here strangers to ourselves.

March 4th 1847

 $\mathcal{T}$his morning, washing the girls' faces with a pan of snow, I said, "Mr. Reed said the Third Relief will be here this week. Maybe a day or two—" I looked up in surprise as Stone entered.

"Good morning, Mr. Stone. I thought Mr. Reed left you at the lake."

"Where's Clark and Cady?" Stone said. He seemed very agitated.

"Mr. Clark has gone hunting with Jean Baptiste. Mr. Cady is sleeping. Is there something wrong?"

Mr. Stone spotted Mr. Cady on the platform and roused him. "There's a bad storm coming," he said.

Mr. Cady immediately began throwing things into his pack.

"What are you doing?" I said. "You're not leaving? Why are you leaving? Mr. Reed said Commander Woodworth is on his way."

They exchanged a look of skepticism and continued packing.

"You can't leave," I said.

"We nearly died coming in here, Mrs. Donner," Mr. Cady said.

"There's not enough food," Mr. Stone said. "It's doubtful Woodworth will ever come—"

"I'll pay you to deliver my children to their sisters at Sutter's Fort."

They looked at each other—panicky, calculating.

"Five hundred dollars," I said.

Mr. Cady abruptly nodded.

I ran outside, crawled into the decrepit wagon just emerged, jabbed at the rusted cleat in the floor, finally unscrewed it, scooped up all the gold coins, ran back, and gave Mr. Cady the money. "I'll pack their things—"

"No, we have to leave now," Mr. Stone said.

"Better count the money," I said, "make sure it's correct. Frances, put more clothes on your sisters and yourself."

I flew around the shelter, frantically gathering items, talking aloud to myself while the coins clinked faster and faster. "The scarlet cloaks for Georgia and Eliza, the matching hoods. Knitted on the Trail, remember? Where's Frances's cloak?" I stuffed three silk dresses, silver spoons into a bag. Put the cloaks and hoods on the girls. "You may wear my shawl, Frances, Momma's big girl, and here's your bluebird hood. Say good-bye to your father now."

The girls stood by George's platform, Georgia and Eliza completely bewildered.

"I love you," George said.

"We must leave, Mrs. Donner," Mr. Cady said.

I tried to adjust Georgia's and Eliza's hoods, pull the shawl closer around Frances. "It may be a while before I see you again, but God and your sisters will take care of you."

"Don't worry, Mother," Frances said. "If we get lost, I'll lead Georgia and Eliza back to you by our foot tracks on the snow."

And then I had all the time in the world to watch the small scarlet and blue shapes trudge behind the men across the snow. Frances is 6 years & 8 months, Georgia 5, and Eliza two weeks shy of 4. "Good-bye," I said, though they couldn't hear me. "Good-bye," I kept saying until my three babies disappeared among the pines.

*F*or days the storm raged. During a small lull, I made it to Elizabeth's and watched her rock Lewis. I kept the fire going, listened to the wind roar. After a long time I said, "You rest awhile, Elizabeth. I'll hold the baby."

I took the dead baby from Elizabeth's arms, laid it on a platform, covered it with a blanket.

Lewis Donner, 3, d. March 7th 1847 at Alder Creek

I led Elizabeth to another platform, lay down next to her, and spooned her body.

"Mrs. Donner, Mrs. Donner." Jean Baptiste shook me, fright on his face.

"Mr. Donner is frantic," Mr. Clark said. "He sent us to find you."

Sammy under Clark's coat, the three of us linked arms and barely made it across the clearing to our shelter.

"Lewis died first," I told George. "Then Elizabeth."

Elizabeth Donner, 38, d. March 8th 1847 at Alder Creek

We brought Sammy over." I placed Sammy next to George for warmth.

Before George woke, I took Sammy from his side, placed my nephew on an empty platform, and covered him.

Samuel Donner, 4, d. March 9th 1847 at Alder Creek

"He's dead," I said to no one or anyone. "They'll all be dead." All night I paced back and forth. "They'll all perish. They can't survive this storm."

Mr. Clark turned over on his pallet. "Try to rest, Mrs. Donner. When the storm breaks, I'll go to the lake camp and see if Stone and Cady made it there with your children."

I rushed through the fresh snow, stopping every few minutes to check my compass, rushed on.

"Your daughters are in Keseberg's shelter, Mrs. Donner," Clark said. "Cady and Stone weren't there. I only looked in the window. Go and stay with them until we can walk out. They may be in great danger. The German is a monster."

"He wasn't a monster before. We all came here strangers to ourselves. Oh God, let my daughters be alive!"

Clark's voice pounded in my ears. "Daughters in great danger, great danger, great danger——" The snow came up to my waist, I fell, dug myself up, fell again, scrambled up, I could see my hands were bleeding but felt nothing. "Please God, please God, please God——"

Inside Mr. Keseberg's cabin, the children sobbed in my arms.

"They threw us in here, Mother," Frances said. "Don't leave us."

"I can stay until rescue comes," I said. "Father sends love."

I held my whimpering daughters as Mrs. Murphy babbled and screamed without stop.

"I will go mad too if she doesn't die soon," Mr. Keseberg said.

Little Simon Murphy had blood smeared on his mouth. A dead child was hung on the wall face to the wall. Its arms were gone. I know who it was, but I can't bear thinking about it.

March 13th—four and a half months trapped in the mountains

I heard them, jumped up and opened Mr. Keseberg's door. Bill Eddy and William Foster, arriving from the west, looked hopefully at me.

"I know my wife is dead," Mr. Eddy said.

"We've come for our boys," Mr. Foster said.

They read the news on my face.

"Our sons are dead," Mr. Eddy said.

Mr. Foster cried out. Tears coursed down both his and Mr. Eddy's cheeks, their grief so raw and deep I had to look away.

James Eddy, 3, died Mar 4th 1847 at lake camp

George Foster, 4, died Mar 7th 1847 at lake camp

Inside the cabin, my daughters clung to me, letting go only to gobble the biscuits that Mr. Eddy gave us, Simon Murphy, and Mr. Keseberg. Mrs. Murphy was too far gone to waste a biscuit on. Mr. Eddy and Mr. Foster could hardly wait to get back outside to the fresh air, and to leave.

"Coming here," Mr. Eddy said, "we passed James Reed. He and the entire Second Relief are in distress. Reed nearly died. The Breens are near death. The Third Relief has gone to succor those still alive."

"I'll give you fifteen hundred dollars if you'll save my children," I said.

"I'll save your children or perish in the effort, Mrs. Donner, but I won't take any money," Mr. Eddy said. "We'll take you also and little Simon Murphy. Mrs. Murphy and Mr. Keseberg are unable to travel."

"Wait till I go back to Alder Creek," I said.

"That's a fourteen-mile round trip, Mrs. Donner. There's another storm coming."

"I must release Jean Baptiste and Mr. Clark from their promise to stay till I returned. I'll hurry."

"Mrs. Donner, there's no great hope of another relief coming in here anytime soon," Mr. Foster said. "It's too dangerous."

"Mr. Donner may have already died, but I can't leave without knowing."

They walked west as quickly as they could. Mr. Eddy carried Georgia. Mr. Foster carried Eliza. Frances and Simon stepped in the men's footsteps. For a while, Frances tried to look back at me, but after she fell the second time, she didn't try again.

I slowly started walking east. I didn't look back.

14th

*I*t was nightfall before I lay down next to George. "Mr. Eddy and Mr. Foster took Frances, Georgia, and Eliza," I said.

"They'll be safe," George said. "I told Jean Baptiste he had fulfilled his promise. He went with Clark."

We lay there in dark and silence.

"We're the only ones here."

"I thought you had gone."

"I haven't fulfilled my promise yet."

He never made a sound. If I hadn't had my hand on his face, I wouldn't have known about the tears.

1829, North Carolina

I was 28 when I met Tully Dozier, not exactly a blushing girl, but the first time I saw him, I knew we would marry. My landlady, the very aptly named Mrs. Folsom, introduced us in her parlor. Mrs. Folsom, at 68, *was* an aging, blushing girl, a woman so filled with romantic notions that were she not so kind and generous she'd have been intolerable. This was the fourth young man she'd way-laid me with in her parlor, the other three barely into long pants.

"Miss Eustis," she called as soon as I opened the door and started toward the stair. "Please join us."

I stood in the doorway through the introductions, a current of electricity flowing between Tully and me so strong that Mrs. Folsom and her other boarders might as well not have been present. I could hardly cross the room and sit down on the settee. I suppose the others conversed, but I simply willed myself to keep my eyes off Tully, and he told me later it was the same for him. How much time passed I don't know, and no verbal signal passed between us, but suddenly he stood up, and as if we were attached I immediately stood up and we walked together out of the room. Mrs. Folsom was beside herself with rapture.

We married three months later. It seemed an eternity to wait.

When Tully died on the grief of my first son and my first daughter, I thought I would die. I very easily could have said good-bye to this earth.

My heart will be pierced when George dies, but no matter how empty or weary I feel, I know now I will not die.

GABRIELLE BURTON

Tully was my first love, the love of youth, and I could never again feel such profound anguish, because the secret of my anguish was my own naïveté.

George is the love of maturity. We came to each other with our eyes wide open and surprised ourselves, finding a fresh, eager space in our tested and scarred hearts.

Last night George pulled my compass out from beneath the platform and handed it to me. "You'll need this," he said. "I rescued it from Georgia and Eliza."

I turned the battered case over in my hand. "I never told you where I got it," I said.

"Yes, you did. Your father brought it from the West Indies."

"That's true. But there's more."

Then I told him about the day Father came home from sea with his leather trunk full of presents, and after everyone had gone to bed, I tiptoed into William's bedroom, past his bed, where he was sleeping soundly, to his desk, and took the compass, and left the conch shell.

"No one ever said anything about it. I was grown up before I confessed to William. He didn't even remember it."

"You've made good use of it," George said.

His remark pleased me enormously, Betsey.

A conch shell cupped to a little girl's ear. Hear the Caribbean Sea. The trade winds. Maybe those warm, blowing winds and the compass needle moving as Father slowly turned around, West of the West, there is a country of the mind, planted the seed for my adventurous spirit and wanderlust.

What does it matter? It is the way I am.

Sometimes, Betsey, I remember your question that I asked George: "Will your wandering feet rest this side of the grave?"

I never answered your question, but George did.

"My movings are over."

I took great care when I slit the threads, but all the pages are loose. Last night my journal slipped from my hands and fell to the floor. Pages everywhere. I put them back in best order I could.

I've always thought that few people have ever seen me as I saw myself, as I really am. It never seemed important as long as I knew who I was. Now as the layers peel off relentlessly, each revealing something unexpected, I've discovered I'm not the person I thought I was. Or is it that I have become a different person? How many layers are there? What if the last layer peels off and instead of some essence refined and distilled and finally revealed, there is nothing there? Perhaps that is what death is.

Or will my soul be there? as I really am

It will be a relief to find out.

Two weeks later

I sit at George's bedside and knit. I am knitting a stocking. Sun comes through the canvas opening. Once, Eliza was there and a sunbeam fell on her lap. She carefully closed her apron around it and brought it to show me, so puzzled when it was gone. It is so quiet and peaceful here, Sister. Everything is unrushed. We have all the time in the world. The only sound is the tiny click of my knitting needles.

"You should have gone with the children," George said.
I put a finger to my lips. "Shhh."

Hooves pounding the ground, mouth frothing, I'm coming, I'm coming, I jump off the horse, run in the farmhouse. "I finally found the doctor in Gulfport, he's on his—" I race past the sobbing hired girl to the still shape on the bed. "Oh, Mrs. Dozier, it was terrible. Mr. Dozier called for you over and over. He died calling your name."
Near the Christmas tree, I bend over Tully, my beloved husband, and weep.

I knit all afternoon until the stocking is nearly finished and I am nearly at the end of my wool. George is watching me. "I never wanted to be one of those waiting women," I said.

At the Harbor young and old women and the children wait silently, tensely, watching the sea as the rowboat moves toward us from the ship farther out in the harbor. I tug at my mother's skirt.

"I always wanted to be one of the ones on the ship," I said. "Going out. Coming back." George smiles and watches me knit. "And so you have been," he says. I smile, finish the skein of wool, unravel the stocking, wind the wool in a skein, and begin to knit again.

I stop awhile at Old Hill Cemetery, where so many Eustises and Wheelwrights lie, go up State Street past Tracy Mansion, how proud we were that Nathaniel Tracy entertained George Washington, John Quincy Adams, Benedict Arnold, a hero then, and *our* grandfather Jeremiah Wheelwright, to Market Square to hear Father clear as day tell us again of the thrilling night they burned the Revolutionary tea, take Federal down to Old South Presbyterian, with Paul Revere's bell and its whispering gallery, you whispering on one side and I on the other until Mother said, That's enough, onto High Street past Knapp House, where we peeped in the windows to see the hand-painted wallpaper that came all the way from Paris, France, past Cushing House, remember, he sailed with Father, stop for a moment to admire Lord Timothy Dexter's house and its splendid cupola, and then, hurrying now, I go around the bend and up the hill to your freshly painted clapboard and there you are, Betsey, your kettle on, eagerly waiting for me.

I found an ox in the snow.

Such a long time since I've eaten meat. At first I gagged and thought I would retch, but I was able to swallow and keep it down. I've had no problem since.

George ate a little too and kept some of it down.

*T*oday I sketched the mountains. Utter silence and solitude, Betsey.

I lift mine eyes to the mountains.

I looked up from my paper. Nearly sunset, an extraordinary golden light filling the sky. Bright and muted shades of gold luminous across the darkening blue. Gold glowing on the snow-covered mountains.

I was rapt.

This echoes the magnificence of our souls.

When I came in, I said, "Where we cut the trees off for firewood, the trunks are beginning to emerge. Spring is coming." And, after a pause, "Would you like to go outside tomorrow?"

The unspoken "for the last time" hung in the air. George looked intently at me, as if gauging both our strengths.

"Very much."

I went out and covered up a partially exposed body.

George leaned heavily on me. In fits and lurches, we proceeded to the log where Jean Baptiste used to prop Georgia and Eliza wrapped up like sausages.

"This is like lugging an ox," George said. "Sure you can manage?"

"I'm sure."

"You're a stubborn woman."

"You knew that when you married me."

"That's *why* I married you."

I helped him sit, sat next to him. He breathed in the fresh air deeply. He looked at the sky in amazement. It was the most vivid blue and seemingly without horizon.

"Now there is a sky to write home about," he said. "They'll never see a sky like that in Illinois."

I nodded in agreement. We sat in silence awhile, then I said, "We don't have the crowding out here either."

Sister, we laughed heartily.

Sitting companionably in the vast expanse, we might have been the only two people alone on the earth together. I knew that behind us lay the shadowed detritus of almost five months of survival, but our view was spectacular and uplifting.

George broke the silence. "I find no place so much to my mind as this."

I turned to him in astonishment.

"You and the children will see things I can't imagine. I'm glad I was part of the beginning," he said. "If I'd stayed home, I would've just gotten older and older. I would've always wondered."

I took his hand and barely breathed out the question that has filled my mind. "Was it too big a price?"

"It's a terrible price," he said, "and it'll never stop costing, and it'll all be worth it. This country is so much bigger than any of us."

Then he looked into my eyes and said, "Wasn't it the biggest, damndest, most thrilling adventure ever, Mrs. Donner?"

"Yes, Mr. Donner, it was."

1846

Thousands of buffalo thunder across the plains, the ground shakes, the sounds rumble through our legs, days off we hear them coming.

The Sioux are on the warpath with the Crow, the fort manager says, they are not happy with the whites either. Off we go in general alarm, quickly overtaken by two hundred Sioux Indians in full war paint. They break into a file of two so that our wagons must pass through them. Elitha and Leanna, if anything happens to Father and me, take our weapons. Eliza, not one peep. We hold our breaths. They take the green twigs held between their teeth and toss them at us. What does it mean? George whispers. I think it's a gesture of friendship, I say.

There's the smell of salt air in our journey, George, we're on a great voyage of discovery, how I wish Father were still alive, I know he would understand.

Mountain men and strange geography and the Irishman fiddling and you and me dancing till the dust flies.

Carving our initials into Independence Rock, where so few have gone before us and so many will come after us.

A 4th of July such as there never was or will be again! Happy 70th birthday, America! Picnic tables groan with food, Elizabeth bakes a dozen gooseberry pies, ex-Governor Boggs orates about Manifest Destiny, that means we're called upon to do this, children, I say, the land waits for us to make it bloom, he's saying that this move west is the best thing ever happened to this country, and we're the ones doing it! George says. This is for all the Springfield boys, Allen Francis said, handing George a bottle of whiskey, but don't touch it till Independence Day of July. Sharp at noon, you Californians turn your faces east. We'll face west and drink to this great country with you. We carefully calculate the time, turn east, and raise our whiskeys and lemonades to our friends in Springfield keeping watch over the East while we open up the West. To the East, to the West, soon to be one United States of America! George says, and we cheer. Then we turn west and cheer again and again until our throats are hoarse from our cheers.

Just the vastness and wonder of our journey and our land. Unlimited possibility, and we a part of history and knowing at the very moment that history is happening and we are helping to make it.

George's polished boots wait by the bottom of his platform.
He doesn't want meat, but I feed him a bit of the last biscuit
James left.

You have enough? he asks.

There's plenty, I say.

There are chunks of oxen, and I haven't even finished my journal
cover.

Today

A ray of sun hits George's gleaming boots.
I offer him a cup of broth.
I'm not hungry, he says.
Just take a sip, I say.
No, thank you, he says.
Through teary eyes, I look at the boots.

Middle of the night

We lie awake next to each other.
He whispers, Thank you for staying with me, my love.
I put my hand on his cheek, say, Sleep well, my darling husband.

I heard a woman screaming in the pines and found myself hitting the ground, my fists bleeding.

I open the coverless Bible to **Deaths** and write,

GEORGE DONNER DIED APRIL 2ND 1847 AT ALDER CREEK AT NIGHTFALL

I light every pinecone and pine kindling torch.

George's body lies upon a platform. I bathe him. Shave him.

The minister asks, Do you take this woman, Tamsen Eustis Dozier, for richer, for poorer, for better, for worse, in sickness and in health, till death do you part?

I hear George say, I do.

I shake out a clean sheet to wrap him for burial.

People stand all around the platform. It's our wedding day. George and I are vigorous, and all the people I love are there, you, dearest only sister, Tully, Baby Tamesin and towheaded Thomas, Jacob and Elizabeth, Elitha, Leanna, Frances, Georgia, and Eliza, all of George's grown children, Allen Francis, Jean Baptiste, Charles Stanton, Milt Elliott . . .

Do you take this man, George Donner—the minister asks.

I turn to George in my wedding dress, I do, I wrap George and tell him, I do, I do.

Frances steps out of the crowd, holding her hand out to me. I hold my hand out to her.

I'm coming, baby.

. . .

I pack the oxen chunk. Unlace George's boots. Crisp the shoe-strings on the fire. Just to be prudent. Responsible people, we made careful preparations. Sometimes your best is not good enough, but that is all you can do. One last entry, Betsey, before I leave this hallowed, godforsaken place.

We are the Donner Party. My husband, George Donner, was the Captain. My name is Tamsen Eustis Dozier Donner. My five daughters are waiting at Sutter's Fort for me. I am bound to go to my children. Almost one year ago to the day, we left Springfield, Illinois, eager to go to California. We have no doubt it will be ad-vantageous for us and for our children. Chain up, boys! Chain up!

AUTHOR'S NOTE

Tamsen Donner never reached California or saw her children again. How she died is unknown. Sometime, possibly two weeks or more after Eddy and Foster left in mid-March with Frances, Georgia, and Eliza, and Tamsen returned to Alder Creek, George died. She wrapped his body in a sheet and set out to cross the mountains.

In mid-April, the Fourth Relief, basically a salvage team, found only one survivor, Lewis Keseberg. The leader, Fallon Le Gros, reported that no traces of Tamsen's person were found, and little of the Donner money they had expected to find, calling Keseberg murderer, robber, and cannibal, charges and taunts that followed him his whole wretched life.

Thirty-two years later, Lewis Keseberg once again proclaimed his innocence, as he had done his whole life, this time to Tamsen's youngest daughter, Eliza. Late one night, he told Eliza, her mother had shown up at his cabin wet, shivering, and grief-stricken, saying, "I must go to my children." He persuaded her to wait until the morning, made a fire, and covered her with blankets. In the morning, he found her dead.

Keseberg had no reason to lie. If he had cannibalized her body, he can't be faulted for it. Tamsen Donner's daughter believed his story and I do too.

Tamsen's journal was never found.

The five Donner daughters lived long lives.

Impatient with Desire is a work of fiction about an actual historic event and real people. By definition, it's a work of imagination, which in some ways suits the subject well, since so few hard facts are known about the Donner Party.

The story of the Donner Party may be the best-known, least substantiated, tale of the nineteenth-century American overland emigration. There are few primary sources and countless contradictory secondary sources, which started to appear soon after the event and continue to the present. The recollections of survivors years later have the strength of personal experience and the weakness of retrospective memory, sometimes confirming another survivor's statement, just as often disagreeing.

Eighty-seven pioneers were trapped in the Sierra Nevada mountains in 1846–47, and every one of them had a riveting story. Unfortunately, almost all of their stories died with them. It is my deep wish that the reader come to see all these people as *real*, their ordeal, almost buried by morbid jokes, become alive.

The novel focuses on one family, George and Tamsen Donner and their five daughters, with the hope that the reader will understand other pioneers through them. The voice is that of Tamsen Donner, a heroine I chanced upon in the early 1970s while writing an apprentice novel about an unrelated subject. A consuming interest in her—obsession would not be too strong a word—began and has continued through decades.

Between numerous other projects, I moved away from Tamsen and back to her, reading widely and deeply on the Donner Party, including the original Patrick Breen diary and many out-of-print books found through rare-book dealers, and corresponding with numerous historians, librarians, and genealogists. Through the courtesy of the Huntington Library, I was privileged to examine letters written by Tamsen Donner, seen by few outside her immediate descendants until recently.

Because I was trying to be a writer and a mother simultaneously, my professional interest in Tamsen Donner became an integral part of our family life:

My husband, five daughters, and I traveled to Newburyport, Massachusetts, where Tamsen was born and grew up.

We went to Elizabeth City, North Carolina, where she taught school, married, became a mother, and in one terrible three-month period lost her first family: her husband, a son, a daughter.

We spent an entire summer retracing the Donner Party's overland route from Illinois to Donner Pass.

We camped, our first time ever in a tent, on Tamsen and George Donner's farm in Springfield, Illinois.

I spent the longest night of my life by myself at the base of the tree where it was believed Tamsen had spent nearly five months in the mountains.

Our kids all became experts on the Oregon/California Trail, dashing off countless school compositions on the subject.

Our dog was named Tamsen.

I wrote an Oregon Trail of words about the Donner Party before realizing that, although I respected historical scholars greatly, I didn't want to write a history of the Donner Party. What I wanted to do was capture Tamsen Donner's spirit.

What I was most interested in was unknown and would never be known: What *really happened* in the more than four and a half months that she was trapped in the mountains with her dying husband and five daughters? What dramas, triumphs, and despairs went on in that tent buried underneath snow? To explore this is to imagine it.

Where possible in the novel, I used historic facts known about the people, route, and dates, although I occasionally deviated slightly for dramatic purposes. For example, William Eustis, Tamsen's father, was actually a sentinel at Old South Meeting House, not Old North Church.

In the attempt to portray real people suffering real tragedy, I speculated, assumed, imagined, ending up with the writer's paradox: moving away from the actual personalities of the Donner Party individuals in the attempt to get closer to their shared humanity with us.

In other words, this is fiction: a lie seeking truth.

I kept the characters' real names in most instances, but not always precisely, because there were a plethora of Williams and Elizabeths/Elithas/Elizas and so forth. Tamsen's sister, Elizabeth Eustis Poor—sometimes Eliza—is Betsey here. Tamsen's sister-in-law, Elizabeth Blue Donner, Betsy in some books, is called her formal name here to lessen confusion.

I took one known fact about Elizabeth "Betsy" Donner—her husband abandoned her with two small boys and she filed for divorce in 1834—and wove a wounded character.

Nothing is known about George Donner's relationship with his brother, Jacob. I took Jacob's character from a single sentence Tamsen's niece Frances Eustis Bond wrote in 1879 to Tamsen's daughter Eliza: "Your Uncle Jake was a sickly, *complaining* man, always had a *whine*."

Doris Wolfinger is invented almost entirely out of whole cloth. I portrayed her as nearly catatonic and crying nonstop, because that seemed plausible behavior for one in her situation. Doris Wolfinger had her personal nightmare within the Donner Party's general nightmare: a new German bride, widowed at nineteen, in a foreign country with no family or friends, unable to speak the language, her husband mysteriously disappeared on the Trail, two of her countrymen his likely murderers. She may well have coped heroically, but that is yet another unknown.

Sometimes I gave known incidents that happened to a different person in the Party to one of the Donner family. Virginia Reed Murphy went buffalo hunting with her father and had to leave her beloved pony behind on the trail; in this story, Leanna Donner does. It's known that the Breens and the Reeds ate their pet dogs; I assume the Donners ate theirs too. I take words from others' mouths—those of Mary Graves, Virginia Reed, Patty Reed—and have a Donner speak them. I did this not to distort history but because it's likely that the Donners did and said similar things. I might have completely rewritten those words into my own fictional versions, but I preferred to keep versions of the original, often heroic, words and deeds alive.

Wherever I could, I used Tamsen's actual words and phrases, such as the description of flowers she saw on the trail, and so on, as drawn from her letters in the following collections: the Sherman Houghton Papers and the Eliza Poor Donner Houghton Pappers, at the Huntington Museum, San Marino, California. The description of the Indians is from the only known letter written on the Trail by George Donner. Elizabeth Cady Stanton, who married one year after Tamsen married George, told the minister to leave out the word "obey" in her vows—I think Tamsen would have approved.

Little is known about Tamsen's childhood. Dorothy Sterling's evocative description in *Lucretia Mott: Gentle Warrior* of Lucretia Mott's childhood nine years earlier in a seafaring community, nearby Nantucket, was a particularly useful source. Frances Bond, Tamsen's niece, told Georgia and Eliza that Tamsen came from illustrious people, but their futures depended upon their own efforts and merits.

For histories and scholarly analysis, I refer the reader to several outstanding current sources to find what facts are now known and continue to be discovered about the Donner Party.

Some may think it's wrong to fictionalize real people. But the saga of the Donner Party, a real historic event, became embellished and distorted almost immediately, passing into social and cultural myth. Why are we so drawn to it? Because it's the American dream turned nightmare? Because we wonder what we would have done had we been there? We make up stories to try to find explanations for mysteries.

If this fiction upsets any descendants or readers, that's the opposite of my intention. To me, almost all the members of the Donner Party, and the California and Oregon emigrants in general, are heroes, even if they didn't always behave heroically. They had strengths and failings because they were complex humans. Every American is indebted to them for opening up the way before us.

BOOKS OF INTEREST

Houghton, Eliza P. Donner. *The Expedition of the Donner Party and Its Tragic Fate.* Chicago: A. C. McClurg & Co., 1911. Reprint, Los Angeles: Grafton, 1920, and Sacramento: Sierra District of California State Parks, 1996.

    Tamsen's baby daughter Eliza, 3 at the time of the emigration, published this book when she was 68. She interviewed many survivors for their versions of what happened in the mountains and has many touching stories about the five Donner sisters after their rescue. I found this book invaluable for tone. Some of Eliza's quotes and two of her stories appear in slightly changed form in the novel. The miniature chair that George made for Georgia was actually made for Eliza by a sympathetic "Mr. Choreman," who expressed his pleasure (159–60) in the words George says. The doll Elitha made for Georgia was made for Eliza, who thought it "perfection" (157). Details of Tamsen's butter molding are from Eliza's description of the butter molding of her caretaker after rescue, "Grandma" Brunner (242). Her husband, Christian Brunner, said that Eliza was his "comfort child" in his troubles (329).

Murphy, Virginia Reed. *Across the Plains in the Donner Party.* Olympic Valley, CA: Outbooks, 1977.

See the following current books and website for the latest Donner Party research and extensive bibliography.

Brown, Daniel James. *The Indifferent Stars Above: The Harrowing Saga of a Donner Party Bride*. New York: William Morrow/ HarperCollins, 2009.

Burton, Gabrielle. *Searching for Tamsen Donner*. Lincoln, NE, and London: University of Nebraska Press, 2009. Contains all of Tamsen Donner's seventeen known letters.

Johnson, Kristin, ed. *"Unfortunate Emigrants": Narratives of the Donner Party*. Logan: Utah State University Press, 1996.

    Also see: www.utahcrossroads.org/DonnerParty: "New Light on the Donner Party," the Donner Party historian Kristin Johnson's exhaustively researched and frequently updated website.

    Also Johnson's blog: http://donnerblog.blogspot.com.

Rarick, Ethan. *Desperate Passage: The Donner Party's Perilous Journey West*. New York: Oxford University Press, 2008.

ACKNOWLEDGMENTS

Leslie Fiedler believed in this book from its nascent beginning, and if he were alive, I know he would be delighted to see that it came to fruition. Sadly, more posthumous gratitude must be given to John Williams and Faith Gabelnick. As I struggled over the years with various incarnations, others who generously gave notes and support were Naomi Weisstein, Ann Petrie, J. R. Salamanca, Nancy Gabriel, Esther Broner, Rose Glickman, and Betsy Rapoport. To true and trusted friends and chance acquaintances, please know I'm grateful, because any work sustained over decades owes its continued existence to a legion of people who say the right word at the right time.

I am indebted to the Henry Huntington Library at San Marino, California, for permission to work with Tamsen Donner's letters, particularly to Peter Blodgett, H. Russell Smith Foundation Curator of Western Historical Manuscripts, and Jennifer Martinez, for their invaluable assistance; and to the Bancroft Library at the University of California at Berkeley for access to Patrick Breen's diary.

Wikipedia was a useful source for information about specimen preservation and cupping. Wikimedia Commons has a trove of public domain botanical illustrations from the eighteenth century.

Thank you to Yaddo and to the MacDowell Colony for their nurturing space and spirit.

Thank you to my editor, Sarah Landis, the copy editor Susan M. S. Brown, Voice managing editor Claire McKean, and the entire Voice/Hyperion team for their belief, enthusiasm, guidance, and care.

Luck came to me in the forms of William Lederer, whose dream inadvertently started me on this journey; Miller Williams, who told me I could be a writer; and Lisa Bankoff, dream agent.

And, finally, what can I say except thank you, again, to Roger Burton, Maria Burton, Jennifer Burton, Ursula Burton, Gabrielle Burton, and Charity Burton, who as artists and family never flagged in their enthusiasm and encouragement.